DOLLOPS

OF

DREAMS

by

SHANTHI RAJASEKARAN
RAJSHRI   RAJASEKARAN

rSr PUBLISHING

Radiant Sunshine Reads

DOLLOPS OF DREAMS

1

JUST ONIONS WILL DO

THE VASUDEVANS' slowly trooped up the stairs as they made their way to their apartment. Mrs. Akila Vasudevan's mind was occupied with the dinner she had to prepare for the night. Mr. Vasudevan's mind was dwelling on the final points of his presentation for the next day's meeting at his office. However, the three little Vasudevans' were in deep argument discussing the Tamil language movie show which they had just returned from.

"Do not look so angry Akka[1] , the songs were quite good ... that guy was really cute," mused Renuka, the second daughter of Mr. Vasudevan.

"Action sequences were terrific" opined Rahul the youngest child of the family.

---

1   Akka-sister(Tamil language)

"Oh gosh that movie is a total waste of time," cried out Geethanjali the eldest daughter of Mr. Vasudevan, sighing in anger and disappointment.

"Open the door Geetha," said her father, handing her the door keys and hoping to divert her thoughts. Turning towards her father she vociferously declared, "I am not coming to watch any more romantic tragedies. Only romantic comedies for me."

"Alright Geetha, open the door first," interrupted her mother.

"I will open," said Rahul reaching out for the keys. Having the keys in their hand and getting a turn to open the door was a prestigious task for the little Vasudevans '.

"I will do it," glared Geetha.

Geetha fumbled with the keys for a moment, as she tried to calm down. The door swung open.

"If the goal is to make us cry, I would rather have cut two dozen onions for you, Amma[2]," she continued turning towards her mother now, "A julienne cut or a diced cut or any other way you want it,"

"And when did you step into the kitchen and ever help me," teased her mother.

"Well... this sure sounds as one benefit of going to this movie," quipped her younger sister.

Before the elder sister could redirect her grumpiness at her younger sister, the mother intervened hurriedly switching on the lights and making her way to the kitchen.

"All right Geetha ...no more tearjerker movies, for you or for us. We will henceforth make sure to go to movies only

---

2 Amma-Mother

where the hero and heroine have a happy ending together and all are smiling with a minimum of 10 pearly white teeth!"

A slightly appeased Geetha stomped her way to her bedroom. There on her bed lay the huge blue Mathematics text book. "Ah, there was a maths test too!" she remembered and moaned.

"Lagrange's Theorem!" she sighed further.

Geetha's father settled down on the sofa in the living room for a brief rest. His two younger children settled down in front of the television.

"Keep the volume low. Your Akka has a test," he observed. And all of a sudden, a happy chuckle drifted from Geetha's bedroom.

"Thank Goodness ...Akka seems to have forgotten that movie," commented Rahul. The father smiled at his son.

"She has a Mathematics test tomorrow," mentioned Renuka.

"Oh yes, Lagrange's theorem," nodded Mr. Vasudevan, aware of the test details too.

"So how is your Science project coming along, Rahul?"

"I am having a problem with the potato battery in trying to make it consistently work,"

"Just write down some numbers to arrive at your conclusion," advised Renuka.

"Akka...!"

"Renuka is just joking, Rahul. Go get your kit. We can try it after dinner,"

"Alright Appa[3]," the son got up and went to his room.

"Renuka," a call came out from the kitchen. "Come and

---

3 Appa-Father

take this coffee for your father,"

"Oh Amma, I am tired, please bring me some coffee too,"

"Renuka...,"

"Alright Amma, coming," got up Renuka wearily and then sat down again, her interest shifting to the advertisement playing on the television

Mrs. Akila Vausdevan slowly entered the room carrying a tray with coffee for her husband and milk for the children. Another chuckle came out of his eldest daughter's room.

"When did our Geetha enjoy Mathematics so much?" Mrs Akila Vasudevan observed to her husband.

"Maybe the movie has made her seek refuge in Mathematics...another good benefit...," commented Renuka.

"And Ms. Wise girl, do you not have anything to study?"

"Amma, this program is interesting. Let me relax for a few moments.I will get to it in a bit."

Mr. Vasudevan smiled and quickly finished his coffee.

"Is this for Geetha? I will take her the milk,"

Carrying the milk gingerly, he entered his eldest daughter's room. And, it was just as he had imagined. The big book of Mathematics lay opened and sprawled and abandoned on the bed. And his dear daughter sat coiled up on a chair beside the bed, hand in hand and immersed in the world of her dear story book 'Arms And The Man' by Bernard Shaw.

"Appa," she looked up sheepishly.

"So Geetha," began the father but before he could continue further, she took the tumbler of milk from him and thrust the book into his hand,

"You really need to read this book first Appa, you will enjoy it too," and then she dreamily rattled on to her father's further surprise and amusement,

"Appa, I am in 11th grade now. After I finish my graduation and then my post-graduation and then when you start looking for a groom for me, please find for me someone like the Chocolate cream soldier hero in this book. Someone as nice and thoughtful like him."

10 SUMMERS LATER

2

LYDIA NOT ELIZABETH

RYAN'S BEST friend and best man was pouring over Ryan's final honeymoon itinerary.

"Thanks Bill! for offering to lend the dough for some of those expenses. I know you guys must be thinking that I am going a bit too overboard with the honeymoon travel expenses but that's what Amanda wanted and I just could not refuse."

"Oh Ryan... let's not talk about it now... we were just concerned when we heard that you have exhausted all of your savings and had to borrow additionally at such an exorbitant rate of interest especially when we know how careful and thrifty you had been all these years."

"True... but the very purpose of saving or earning is to

meet the needs of our near and beloved ones. There is no greater joy than to be able to shower our soulmate all that she asks."

"Ryan, these are not needs. These are wants!" interjected another friend and then regretted his words as Ryan's face momentarily lost it's brightness and his other friends scowled at him.

"All right, we are not holding an economics lecture now."

"Well, Amanda is one lucky girl"

"But we cannot still fathom that this is happening now. You are the first in our friends circle to tie the knot and that too so early. It was just a few months ago that you completed your medical residency"

"You never had a single girlfriend even in the college days and never went out on dates... always glued to your books and ambition to become a doctor"

At that moment, the door burst open and a jolly old lady rushed into the room

"Ryan my dear nephew...Congratulations!" gushed Aunt Agatha embracing Ryan.

"Aah... Aunty, finally you are here. Even yesterday we were worrying if there will be a delay in your schedule in reaching Miami. So how was your cruise?"

"Oh, forget all that Ryan...we have bigger things to catch up on!"

"Wow Ryan, I'm so...so happy for you. Tell me all about your Amanda. I'm just a bit surprised that all these years you never breathed a word about her... That you had a sweetheart in school itself..."

Ryan looked a little perplexed.

"Oh Aunty...," interjected Bill. "It is true that we all went to the same school and were in the same class too for quite some years. But our paths were different and we do not recall my friend ever having interacted with her. She belonged to a different group totally."

It was Aunt Agatha's turn to be puzzled.

"Well aunty" Ryan started to explain with a smile "It was this January that we were really brought together. Amanda's father had a heart surgery and I was one of the doctors taking care of him...,"

And before he could continue, the merry Aunt filled in the dashes.

"Alright so one thing led to another... And here we are today, "

"Yes, and while her father got cured, his daughter and the doctor got afflicted by the supreme love bug!" added his friends laughing merrily.

Aunt Agatha looked at Ryan's face flush with happiness.

"On Ryan... I am so happy for you. I just can't wait to meet her... Last week in our book reading club session on the cruise, we were reading Jane Austen's 'Pride and Prejudice.' All through the session I remembered how it was your one real favorite book and you had even gone so far to say that when you settle down ...you will look for someone like Elizabeth Bennett. So, I am so happy that you have found the Elizabeth Bennett of your dream"

"Elizabeth Bennett...the room erupted in laughter. She is more like Lydia Bennett cried all his friends' voices in unison.

For a fleeting second, a strange sense of nervousness

and uneasiness trigged Ryan's heart. Well it's just the usual pre-wedding jitters, he assured himself and joined his friends' playful banter.

3

THE RAIN GODS ARE CRYING

THE RAIN starved city of Chennai was all of a sudden blessed with copious amounts of rain.

Mr. Vasudevan, the father of the bride grandly strode with pride and happiness through the wedding hall, surveying the arrangements and meeting the guests.

"A monsoon in the month of April? Unbelievable!" commented the guests as they entered the wedding hall. The bride was sending prayers every other minute to the Gods. She was not praying for her future happiness. She forgot all about that. She was only praying,

"Let everything go smoothly. Let my dad be happy. Let the guests come. Let the vegetable delivery vans come on time to prepare the wedding meals. Let none of my dad's wedding arrangements go in vain."

The bride's prayers did not go unanswered. Mr. Vasudevan's wedding arrangements did not go in vain. All of the invited guests, trooped in as expected, unaffected by the rain. The special vegetable truck from Ooty arrived. As one Mr. Kannapan and his family entered the marriage hall, Mr. Vasudevan's smiles almost reached his ears. They were the members of the most influential and wealthy family back in his native town.

"All the Lords and Lordesses of our native town are here, Geetha," he gushed.

The bride heaved a sigh of relief. But all was not rosy. Reports of the bridegroom mother's behavior soon reached the bride's dressing room. And they were not very pleasant to digest.

"Come on Geetha ...focus here, whatever are you thinking about and having a worried face now? We still have the makeup to do," called out her cousin sisters.

Her Aunt Mrs. Narmada walked into the dressing room carrying a bag.

"Where is Aunty bringing the bag from?" she wondered. Surely it was in the room already earlier.

"And here are the jewels," cried out her Aunt with a smile. For a brief second Geetha saw her father's face begin to tense. But it relaxed, as her aunt nodded her head beaming in his direction.

"Oh Geetha ...I forgot to tell you, but please do not take it to heart. I knew you wanted to have the recital of the marriage rites in the Tamil language, but unfortunately due to the rains, that priest was not able to come."

Oh, so Appa was just worried for this, thought Geetha

with relief. As she was made to settle down and the bridal makeup began, Mrs. Sushmita Ravindran the mother of the bridegroom stormed into the room. Geetha got up in respect. But the lady hardly cared to acknowledge her. She just addressed her aunt with a booming voice.

"The jewels you showed now were all fine. But we did not check the necklace and bangles which the bride is already wearing."

"Actually, we have the receipts for those,"

"Oh, how will we know for sure that those are the receipts for these exact pieces of jewelry. Let's just check them directly,"

"Certainly Sambandhi[4]," her Aunt demurely murmured.

"Geetha, please give your jewels for a few minutes," she whispered apologetically to Geetha.

The lady had apparently brought along with her a goldsmith to check on the authenticity of the gold and to verify the quantity of sovereigns of gold that Mr. Vasudevan was gifting his daughter with.

The weighing scale was produced. Geetha's stomach churned. She turned away. The examination was completed. The lady and her goldsmith strode out of the room importantly.

"Here Geetha take the bangles back."

"Oh Geetha, why are your hands trembling? Did you not have your breakfast?"

"Let me put on the necklace carefully. It will upset your hair-do"

---

4 Sambandhi-Relationship term to address the mother of the bridegroom

The bride felt her chest tightening as she felt that necklace back on her . For the first time that day, she began to think of her life. For the first time she remembered that she had forgotten to pray to God for a happy married life for herself.

Mrs. Shyamala, another aunt of Geetha's took her hand and tried to hold it comfortingly.

It's all right. Ashok will be different. He will be good, Geetha's tried to comfort herself slowly. Oh, will he be really different... searched her inner voice feverishly. It was just 45 minutes for the muhurtham[5] . Geetha's eyes followed the movement of the pendulum on the clock ticking away. "There's no time to panic now," she mused.

The muhurtham time arrived. Geetha was led down the marriage hall. She took another glance at her father. He stood blissfully happy. "Well Geetha, do not fear" her mind reassured her. "Your father will always do only what's good for you." Geetha took her place beside the bridegroom. She looked towards him in anticipation. It was not like in the movies. He did not look for a second in her direction. He appeared to be preoccupied in talking to his family members while mechanically following the instructions provided by the priest conducting the ceremony. And then he did look up. But it was not in her direction. She followed his eyes. It appeared to rest on a girl seated in the wedding crowd. The bride looked away in disappointment. Like a little girl lost in a fair, she again searched for her father's face. He had the same blissfully happy look.

"It's alright. Your father would have surely checked up

____

5   muhurtham-Auspicious time of the day to conduct the wedding ceremony

on him. Your father would always do only what is good for you," her mind reiterated.

The rites continued. And then that moment arrived. The beats from the mathalam[6] and the music from the nadhaswaram[7] reached a crescendo. All the guests rose from their seats showering rice blessings and flowers on the couple. Ashok tied the Thali [8]around her neck She no longer was Geethanjali Vasudevan. She was Geethanjali Ashok.

She again turned towards the man who had now officially entered her life with anticipation. He was busy answering something to his mother and sister. They were left with the final rites of walking around the fire. Geetha fondly remembered the significance behind the practice as explained in the Tamil work of literary art named Thirupaavai . The loving but firm hold grasp with which the husband takes and holds his newly wed wife's hands signifies the extent of his care for her.

Geetha held out her hand demurely and Ashok took it. And then Geetha's stomach churned again. Her chest tightened again. As they took their steps around the fire, her whole being quivered. She just could not mistake it. It was a lackluster, namesake hold devoid of any feeling. She watched the flames from the ceremonial fire in a trapped trance. Were her dreams being burnt? Who is this man? cried out her heart. Appa! Where is my chocolate cream soldier?

3 SUMMERS LATER

4

ARTIFICIAL TEARS PLEASE

THE OPHTHALMOLOGIST picked up his prescription pad and looked questioningly in Geethanjali's direction. "Ms. Geetha....," he began to write her name on the prescription.

"Ms. Geethanjali Vasudevan," she helped him with her name.

"Alright Geethanjali. I have prescribed you, artificial tear-drops. Do you work long hours on the computer?"

"Not really doctor. I have just started working very recently."

"And some omega-3 tablets," saying he tore off the prescription and handed it over to Geethanjali.

"It's just a case of dry eyes."

"Thank you doctor."

The niece Geethanjali and her aunt both thanked the doctor and got up to leave

Geetha and her aunt Mrs. Shyamala walked out of the doctor's office to the reception.

Mrs. Shyamala Sundaram, here is your bill. And Ms. Geethanjali Vasudevan, here is your bill," handed out the clerk at the reception counter.

"Thanks Geetha for accompanying me to the doctor today, "

"Oh aunty... Not at all. And because of coming along with you I was able to show my eyes too to the doctor."

"But Geetha, I'm surprised that you are having dry eyes at this young age."

"Well aunty, in the last three years... I have cried so much that my tear glands itself must have got fed up and stopped functioning. So, I need artificial tears now," replied Geetha trying to find humor in her situation.

But as much as she tried, she could not feign a smile. Her aunt looked up and saw those red tired eyes. She was afraid of upsetting her niece but could not control herself.

"What have you been doing Geetha? Are you not sleeping well?"

"I just cannot sleep aunty," admitted Geetha,

"Geetha?"

"I am scared to sleep..., It's fear of the future... I'm scared as to how I'm going to carry on like this forever."

"Geetha..."

"I'm scared as to how long will my parents support me. A divorced daughter is not a welcome addition to most homes. How long will I be able to bear this cursed existence."

"Just scared," her voice broke down to a fearful whisper and she looked away.

"Geetha," her aunt gently touched her hand, "Have you heard of the saying –Take baby steps? Taking up a job will be the first baby step that you can take to find some sense of turnaround in your life. Be brave, Geetha. Just be brave."

The niece nodded slowly.

5

CAREFREE SMILE

THE SMALL hospital cafeteria resounded with the joviality of two young ladies exchanging girlish banter on the happenings of the weekend. For a moment it pierced Geetha's train of thoughts and made her pause as she picked up her morning breakfast. It was her second week of joining work at the hospital. She being an MBA had joined the administration team in the hospital. She had taken up the job as a first step towards the second innings of her life. But it was hardly stress relieving in any form for her yet. It only awakened her more to her plight. She felt tortured by the prying questions from the curious new colleagues in her department on her marital status and current background.

"Oh, you're a widow," had suggested one colleague in return to her evasive answers and she had to finally admit that she was a divorcee.

"Oh God! How am I going to face them each day? What is in store for me today?" she thought as she picked up her bag and made her way out of the cafeteria door.

"I need to collect my ID card" she remembered and made her way to the admin officer, Mr. Ganesh, just in time to hear the words from a new voice,

"Such an innocent, carefree smile. But this is surely not me." And he put down the card on the desk.

"Oh, I'm extremely sorry. I mixed up the cards" apologized Mr. Ganesh and handed another card saying, "This is your card doctor"

"Thanks..." smiled the young doctor, "And I will make sure not to misplace my card again"

"And doctor, these are the tickets for the evening flight and the complete schedule of your trip to the Delhi seminar for this week. Please just sign these couple of forms"

"Which, state in USA are you from Doctor?" Mr. Ganesh began chatting as he handed the forms.

"Florida...the sunshine state," answered the doctor genially. As the young doctor pulled out his pen, his phone too rang.

Mr. Ganesh then noticed Geetha, waiting quietly in the background.

"Hello Mam, here is your card," he greeted pulling up the card on the desk.

Oh... was this not the same card that the doctor had laid down on the desk? thought Geetha realizing with surprise that the doctor had apparently commented on her very ID card. She looked back in the direction of the doctor. She could not see his face. His head was bent and he was quite busily engrossed on the phone. Dr. Ryan Richardson M.D read the name tag on the doctor's white coat.

"And mam you're finally been assigned your desk. It is just in the corner of this hall."

"Thanks," said Geethanjali. The day was probably going to be allright. And she mechanically began to thrust it into her handbag. And then the doctor's words faintly resonated in some corner of her head. What had evoked that response from that doctor? Which photo had she submitted for her ID card? She curiously pulled out her ID card back again. She looked at the face beaming out of the picture. It was a picture taken approximately four years ago on the convocation of her MBA graduation. Yes, it was a day when she had been deliriously happy, held high dreams of the future and had felt on top of the world. She wanted to be that girl all over again.

"Is that ever possible?" she thought with misgiving. She looked up again to look for the doctor. But he was not there. He had apparently left.

"Thank you, Mr. Stranger, for helping me remember one of the nicer days," she could not help thanking him in her mind.

6

ONE EVENING...

GEETHA SAT impatiently observing the minute hand of the clock hung across the hallway.

The deep gongs from the bells of the church clock slowly but surely resounded across the hallway. Geethanjali had long before shutdown her desktop. She had had a really long day. In fact, the entire week had been grilling and she was actually feeling a bit important and busy. Her supervisor had actually commended her on the reports that she had compiled and prepared for that month's operations. And after three months of service as a trainee, she was now confirmed as an employee. So, she did have quite a bit of news to carry with her to home. Grabbing her bag she hurried down the hall to the elevators.

"Ullathil Nalla Ullam Urangaa Thenbathu
Vallavan Vaguthathadaa Karna,
Varuvathai Ethirkolladaa..."[9]

Sang out her phone ring tone. Geetha pulled out the phone from her bag and saw that it was her mother calling and she smiled. Oh, probably she was calling to hurry her home. She may have planned some mini celebration for her as she had already shared her the good news of being confirmed as an employee.

"Amma... I'm on my way. I should be there in another 30 minutes," answered Geetha as she pressed the elevator button.

"Geetha...," hesitated the voice on the other end. And then it continued

"Geetha, can you please buy some butter beans on the way home.?"

"Amma, butter beans have not been available for the last two weeks...," Geetha began to say. However, she was interrupted by her mother,

"I'm not saying about the shops in our area. I'm talking about Pandian vegetable shop in Mylapore. It will surely have it."

"But Amma, it is already 6 o'clock. If I go to Mylapore now during the peak traffic hours, it will be a whole couple of hours before I get back home"

"There is also a parayanam[10] in the temple there at around

---

9   Ullathil Nalla ...The words of a song from a Tamil movie named Karna-The literal meaning is -The good soul ,would never sleep and would face whatever is coming

10   parayanam-religious discourse

7 pm. You can attend that as well" continued the voice hesitatingly on the other end.

Why was her mother giving her these strange tasks for the evening? And then it dawned on Geetha. She was not wanted at home on time.

"All right, what time will everyone be gone? When do you want me back at home?" she interrupted her mother. There was a pause.

"9 o'clock should be fine. What can we do? We only got the information now that the bridegroom's family had got the 'OK' from their astrologer a short while ago and today being an auspicious day they wanted to come in today itself"

"All right, Amma... No need for explanations. I will get your butter beans tomorrow and tonight I will come in after 9 pm. I have lots of work to do at office itself," saying she hung up the phone. The elevator door opened, waited and closed.

She slowly pulled her way back to her desk with troubled thoughts.

The prospective bridegroom's family were coming in that evening to see her younger sister Renuka. Although Geethanjali was the elder sister she was not wanted to be present on the occasion as it would raise uncomfortable questions on her marital status. Her parents were concerned that Geethanjali's failed marriage should not affect her younger sister's marriage prospects.

"Is it my fault that I married the wrong man in the first place? And is it wrong that I tried to break free from that mess?" her heart pained.

"Hey, cheer up... Things are actually improving... Before you had to go rushing to the temple or library and spend hours there whenever these meetings or family occasions were held. Now you have a workplace to wait out the time." reasoned out her mind.

Nevertheless, she felt a tug at the heart. This was not new to her. She had gone through this banishment many a time. But still she had not become wholly immune and it continued to hurt her as she tried to reason out that it wasn't her fault that she had been married to one of the wrong creations of mankind. Her face turned pale. Her steps turned heavy as she slowly dragged herself across the hallway. She quickly looked around and felt relieved that no one was around. The floor was deserted and everyone working on that floor had already left for the day. She passed by the kitchen and stopped. Maybe I should get some water she thought and retraced her steps back into the kitchen. She filled the bottle mechanically with some water. Trying to calm her thoughts she began to slowly sip some water. As she sipped the water she managed to smile. Hmmm... The doctor's eye medicine is still not working. I'm not getting any tears or maybe it's better that it does not work. At least I will not make a fool of myself by crying outwardly.

Feeling a little better she shut her eyes "Oh God... Can you please help turnaround this miserable existence. Or at least please give me the courage to become immune to this kind of alienation."

And suddenly, she was jolted out of the thoughts by the shrill notes of a cell phone ringing. Opening her eyes, she looked at her hand. It was not her phone. It was coming from elsewhere but sounded very near.

Whoever can it be? She had thought there was no one in

the floor of the hospital. She came out of the kitchen and looked around. Yes, no one was to be seen. But the rings were sounding very close to where she was standing. The phone ring ceased for a brief second before it rang again. Again, Geetha's eyes swept the room, the floor, the kitchen counter but no phone was to be seen. The ringing stopped. And then it rang again. Well only the refrigerator is left she thought and pulled open the door. And yes... lo and behold... there it was... a black shiny phone ringing loud and clear. She hesitated for a moment but the incessant ringing, plodded her to answer it. Before she could even finish saying a "Hello" a frantic, excited voice on the other end spoke out,

"We are calling from the hotel SkyTowers. Mrs Agatha Robertson had been found in an unconscious state a short while ago by the housekeeping staff. She has been rushed to the nearby hospital Mt Carmel. You have been given as an emergency contact for Mrs. Robertson. Please come in immediately."

7

MRS ROBERTSON

IT WAS after three long hours following Geethanjali's arrival, that Mrs. Robertson was moved to the hospital room from the emergency ward. The duty doctor followed by the nurse entered the room. The last of the test results had been obtained.

"As we suspected before, the tests confirm that this is just a case of bad food poisoning. So, nothing to worry."

"Doctor, you earlier said her BP was high too," reminded Geetha.

"We have controlled it now. The nurse will bring some medication later too, She is just badly dehydrated and needs a lot of liquids. She should be fine after this last bottle of drip"

"When can she eat doctor?" Geethanjali inquired. She kind of recalled the old words of wisdom that one may need to starve during a food poisoning attack but was wary if Mrs. Robertson would be able to manage without food.

"Well, she can eat a small light meal if she feels hungry. It's just important that she needs to drink fluids. The vomiting and diarrhea has made her very weak."

After filling a few other forms, the doctor and nurse left the room. Geethanjali turned towards Mrs. Robertson. The lady was looking extremely pale. Added to it, Geethanjali found the lady squinting her eyes and looking at her. Poor lady, maybe she does not trust me or understand that I'm from her nephew's hospital thought Geethanjali and slowly moved towards her. The lady's squinted look continued.

"Mrs. Robertson... I know how you must be feeling uneasy to be in the midst of strangers in a hospital room... but please be assured that I'm from your nephew's hospital. Here is my identification card from the hospital," said Geetha pulling out her identification card.

"Oh no my child...," cried out the old lady. "I've been watching how you handled everything for me and I will be eternally thankful for your thoughtful help and support this night... I never for a moment doubted you my child."

And then the reason for Geethanjali's question and response dawned upon her and she slowly sheepishly smiled. And also, the color and spirits returned to her face, as she burst out laughing tearing down the formality between them.

"I'm afraid I just cannot see that well without my glasses. In fact... if I do not squint, I see everything kind of magnified ..... Not sure what happened to my glasses when they brought me in. But it's okay, I do happen to have another spare one at the hotel."

"Oh," understood Geetha relieved too "If you can tell me the exact location and give me the authorization to enter your hotel room I could easily fetch them for you right away."

"That would be so helpful Geetha...but it's already so late for you and these last few hours must have been hectic for you."

Yes, those last few hours had been pretty hectic for her as she had waited outside the intensive care unit, trying to catch hold of her hospital admin manager, trying to trace the staff to whose phone it belonged and then trying to locate that hospital staff only to find out that it was a doctor who was on a flight to Delhi for a seminar and would probably be a couple of days before he gets back.

"Oh, that's all right Mrs. Robertson. I know how tough it is to manage without glasses"

And then it was Geetha's turn to start laughing as a picture of her uncomfortable, pained little brother's face struggling to read those boring newspapers came floating to her memory.

"Oh Mrs. Robertson ... I recall how my little brother had once sat on the glasses of my uncle and he was so furious with him and so miserable without the glasses. As a punishment, my then little eight year old brother had to skip his playtime and was made to read the newspaper from beginning to the end for my uncle without skipping a single section."

"Oh my!" Mrs. Robertson burst out laughing as she too tried to visualize a little boy with a pained expression reading the newspaper end to end.

The door then opened. And in came the ward boy wheeling the trolley with some food, followed by the nurse and doctor again.

Geetha was amused to see the new expression on Mrs. Robertson's face. "Food, finally..." she whispered with a chuckle to Geetha

"Oh good you are laughing," smiled the doctor.

"Your BP is almost normal."

"Oh, good Doctor. What was it before?"

"Well, that was around 260 then. Anyways, you can have this porridge and then have this medicine. We will review tomorrow again." saying he strode out of the room. The nurse took a seat in the back of the room.

"260...that's pretty high, I remember taking my medicine in the morning. What made it go so high? Was it just my diarrhea?" she pondered.

"Oh...," she recalled and then her face flashed angrily. She caught sight of Geetha's alarmed face and mellowed down helplessly.

"What can I do Geetha...when I think of what I heard today, it makes my blood boil over!" She paused and then began to explain.

"I had a very dear old friend back in Florida, who had relocated back to India some years ago. She was one of the primary reasons to light this travel bug within me to come and explore India. Today afternoon, we had planned to meet for a coffee and a good old chat. But instead, I got a call from her where she was sobbing hysterically that she was standing outside the emergency room of an hospital with her sister. Her nephew had committed suicide and was lying on the hospital bed while the parents were battling and begging God, the doctors and all and sundry for their son's life.

"How callous some children can be nowadays?" she

declared.

"Callous?" Geetha was surprised. That was a strong word for someone who had just got a fresh lease of life.

"Yes callous, irresponsible or selfish or plain foolishness," she seethed. The nurse looked up from her book.

"He was a fine young man of 20 years with a loving family and still in college and fighting fit physically. So can you guess, what made this foolish boy suddenly feel that all was over in this world?"

"Exams ...?" asked Geetha slowly, "He failed in his exams ...?"

"Exams...?" Mrs. Robertson looked incredulous.

"Well for some students, exams and studies mean the world to them over here, especially when they view that as the sole rope to come up in life. But by your look, I guess that is not the case here ...,"

"Oh true...not for exams in his case..,"

"It must be failed love then ...," guessed Geetha again

"Yes ...that's right. Unrequited love from some girl. Yes, unrequited love will be painful. But was he born in this world just for that sole purpose? Did he even know that girl when he was an infant in his mother's womb or when he took his first walk or spoke his first word? Why on earth does he need to pay such importance to the love of one such human being."

"Strange is the way of the human mind. So many thoughts.. So many dreams. So many pressures. So many influences. And then some passions, some disappointments, some setbacks and kind of makes the thoughts messy...,"

"No Geetha...," she dismissed Geetha's thought process.

"That love for the girl should just, at the most be one finished chapter in his life. Not the entire life."

"There is just not one day that the Sun bestows on us for our whole life. Every day sets into a night. And after every night dawns a fresh day."

"Oh Mrs. Robertson...take it a little easy. I am not giving excuses for his behavior."

And then she slowly added. "But then he's just 20 years you say. So, guess he lacked the emotional intelligence or maturity to see the bigger picture. They say the human brain does not fully mature until a little later."

"Mam have you finished your porridge? You need to take your medicine soon after it," interrupted the nurse.

"Oh sorry," murmured Mrs. Robertson and opened the lid

"I suppose that's true. He has not been exposed to the real experiences in life. Not everyone are so immature at his age. Anyways ...he needs some help I suppose," she sighed herself and took a sip of the porridge

"Arrgh....!" she let out a cry. "I need some help. Whatever is this food nurse? My BP will surely rise now ...," she managed a feeble joke.

But the nurse was not very amused. And just gave a nonchalant look and returned to the book she was reading.

"Well isn't that what life is all about? One day, it is all bright and shiny with lofty hopes and dreams and then the next day the dreams and hopes may look a little bleak, and then the very next day it may more dismal, but then a few days later the hopes and dreams will take shape again ...,"

"Mam, it's getting late for your medicine," interjected the

nurse.

"Allright, I am done. I am not hungry anymore. In fact, I am just tired and sleepy." She let out a yawn.

"Let me get started right away as you settle down for some sleep," got up Geetha with a smile as the old lady gave out yet another yawn.

"And in case you're asleep when I return, I will leave the glasses in the top drawer of the night stand by your bedside" continued Geetha getting up ready to leave.

"Oh, it's already late for you. You should rather bring it in tomorrow instead."

"Alright, Mrs. Robertson,"

"Good night, my child"

"Good night, Mrs. Robertson. Take care."

8

EMERALDS ARE ALWAYS LUCKY

"Amma, take a sip and tell me. Is it spicy in anyways? Is the salt sufficient?"

Mrs. Vasudevan slowly tasted the rasam[11] which her daughter had offered. "No Geetha, it's not spicy. In fact, I can hardly taste the pepper. And the salt is just right. It's very nice Geetha." concluded Mrs. Vasudevan.

She was very relieved to see Geetha being occupied and looking so cheerful. She had been fearful that her daughter would have been upset for having had to avoid her younger sister's bride seeing ceremony in the previous evening.

"But why are you making rasam now. Are you not going to eat in the cafeteria today?" asked Mrs. Vasudevan.

"This is not for me Amma. This is for Mrs. Robertson the lady whom I was telling you about last night. I did check out the food options in the hospital and they did not seem to be too promising. She needs bland but nourishing food. Thus, I'm preparing rasam in grandmother's style. And just imagine, how dreadful it would be to stay alone with no family around you in a hospital."

Mrs. Vasudevan did not have anything to say to that. She vaguely remembered that her daughter had been trying to tell her something about a lady the previous night. But she had hardly registered the details then as she had been mentally preoccupied with the happiness and details around the fixing of her second daughter's alliance.

Her mind again switched over to her second daughter's alliance. She heaved a happy sigh!

"We have a lot of things to be done in a very short time. The engagement is fixed for next week. And you know how Renuka is so choosy. She will make us climb the steps of umpteen shops and will keep changing her mind, before she decides what she truly wants and then get it."

"I could help Amma. I love shopping," volunteered Geetha excitedly and then regretted it.

"Oh, you have your work to go to," dismissed her mother gently.

"True, Amma," she agreed readily to the excuse. She should have known better. She surely was not wanted in any place or activity that was for auspicious reasons.

And then the new bride to be walked into the kitchen, stifling a yawn.

. "Oh Amma... do not fear. I have the almost perfect plan already in place."

Geethanjali switched off the stove and turned towards

the younger sister fondly with eager questions. How time flies she mused. Her little sister was all grown up and soon going to be married. She had not been able to get an alone moment with her younger sister the previous night. Renuka, had been busy in her room chatting on the phone with her friends giving them the details of her alliance.

"Congratulations Renu!" greeted Geethanjali.

"Thanks, Akka."

"So Renu...tell me all about...." began Geethanjali. But Renuka interrupted her with her own question "Akka, can I have your emerald set, necklace and bangles?"

Geethanjali turned speechless on hearing her request. Her emerald set...she thought confusedly. Wasn't that her favorite pretty jewelry set ? The one she had personally chosen when her father had wanted to gift jewelry for her graduation... How could she possibly just give it away so simply... ?

She managed to find her voice and slowly began, "But.. I..." Before she continued, she was again stung by her sister's next statement. "Oh Akka, what is the hesitation? You surely have no use for it anymore."

Geethanjali turned helplessly towards her mother. Her mother avoided looking at her. But she could sense the feeling of consternation in her mother's countenance. Poor Amma. Which daughter could she be expected to support?

And then Mrs. Vausdevan slowly turned towards Geethanjali with downcast eyes.

"Geethanjali..." she began to say.

"It's in the bank locker Amma. I will bring it home on Saturday." volunteered Geethanjali.

A joyous event was going to take place in the family after a long time. She did not want to cloud anyone's happiness.

"All right that's settled then." smiled Renuka and started rattling away the next item on her wish list.

"Amma, do you recall that green brocade saree advertisement in the magazine that I showed you. I think that would be perfect with the emerald set"

"Oh Renu. You're always showing dresses in the magazines.... which one is this now? "

"Amma... It was just two days ago,"

Geethanjali turned away from the banter. "At least they do not consider your jewelry unlucky." a voice teased her from within.

She turned towards the stove. She did not want to spend the day with anymore sad thoughts. She turned on the stove and watched the rasam boil over.

9

MR STRANGER INDEED

A WEEK LATER on a bright Sunday afternoon, a sprightly old affable Mrs. Robertson greeted Geethanjali in the reception of the hotel where she was staying.

"Oh Geetha... So glad you could make it," she clasped her hands in happiness.

Geetha was amused to see her exuberant self. What a welcome contrast to the pale, feeble face that had peeped out of those white hospital sheets.

"Ryan is finally back!"

"Oh," smiled Geetha. "Guess, that's the reason for the happiness on your face,"

"Well, that's because I am finally off all those medications and feel like my old self again "

"Come on in. Ryan was waiting to see you and extend his

gratitude."

"Oh Mrs. Robertson... There's no need for another thank you. But why are we going into the restaurant?"

"Well this is our small token of thanks...a surprise lunch for you. Both of us do not have the skills or the ability to cook up delicious home-cooked food like you have treated me with at the hospital and even after coming back to the hotel."

Geetha found herself propelled into the restaurant as Mrs. Robertson refused to listen to her polite refusal.

"We will take the corner table." she said to the hostess.

They passed by the pianist just settling down.

"Oh good, there's piano music too today for lunch, probably since it's a weekend." mused Mrs. Robertson as they settled down in their places.

"We will order a little later. We are expecting another person." she dismissed the waiter. Turning towards Geetha she added, "Ryan had to take a phone call. He should be here any moment."

Geetha nodded her head quietly. She suddenly started feeling a little nervous and self-conscious. She was going to meet a senior doctor at her hospital. Mrs. Robertson was a very friendly lady and Geetha had enjoyed being around her the last one week. But how was her nephew going to be? Generally, her hospital would sponsor only the very senior doctors for a workshop or a seminar. Would he thus be an absent-minded, brilliant but stern doctor who had to politely put up with his aunt's guest.

She watched with trepidation, an old man in possibly his late 50s with the same color of hair and eyes as Mrs.

Robertson walk into the restaurant. "Is he the one?" she thought dismally. As feared, he did not have any pleasant, amiable facial appearance but a rather surly and grim look.

"Hello Ms Vaudevan," a warm voice sounded from behind breaking into Geetha's thoughts. She turned back to see a tall and quite handsome man in his early 30s' and strikingly kind blue eyes and a very genial smile on his face. "So glad to meet you," said Mrs. Robertson's nephew and stretched out his hand to shake hers.

All her uneasiness vanished. As pleasant as his aunt, she thought as he pulled out his chair and sat down with them.

"Ryan Richardson," he continued, "I guess we have not had the opportunity to meet before."

There was something vaguely familiar about him or his name to Geetha, but she could not quite place it then.

"Firstly many, many thanks for all the care which you showed towards my aunt in the hospital."

"Please Dr. Richardson... It was just something that we all will automatically do. When we work at the same place, we are bound to help each other as coworkers if any need arises. It's not special."

"For a coworker whom you have never interacted with and to rush out in the night... That was indeed special."

"Well hope you feel that your Aunt's recovery is satisfactory. "

"Feel fit as a fiddle." interjected Mrs. Robertson. "Ready to go off on my next trip."

"Sorry aunty. No more jaunting around for some time. Have you not learnt a lesson and have had enough?" asked a shocked Ryan.

"Ryan... It was unfortunate that I had to suffer from bouts of food poisoning. But the travel bug is only still stronger. I can still never forget the last trip to Thanjavur. The magnificent Big temple is still looming before my eyes...You must have surely been there Geetha"

"I was a little too young when I visited that Temple with my family. Thus, I barely remember the details. The only place that I kind of remember is probably Mamallapuram which is just here near Chennai."

"Well see these pictures....," saying Mrs. Robertson, flipped out her phone and shared the pictures around and started recalling the facts that she had heard about the temple.

"Of course, the pictures do not do justice to all that glory. You need to see it in person. When I stood there, I had a very humbling, peaceful experience. I just felt like relocating to that little town so as to be able to visit that Temple frequently." she continued.

"I heard so many fascinating facts on how the foundation was laid. The names of every single artisan or common man who contributed in anyways to the building of the temple have been inscribed there!"

Ryan smiled at his aunt's enthusiastic account. She further continued, "Do you know that the King Raja Raja Chola who built this temple was one of the greatest emperors of all in his lifetime. He had such a strong naval force in those days." She turned expectantly towards Geetha, expecting her to regale his conquests too.

Geetha smiled slowly, "Well, he may have once been a mighty conqueror. But, those boundaries have changed. As we all see, what stands the test of time is one's contribution towards creations. His Temple is a masterpiece and is the eternal real gift to humanity."

And then she paused as she saw the aunt and nephew looking surprisedly at her viewpoint.

"Well Geetha about Mamallapuram that you mentioned... that name rings in a bell. Yes, that's in my list of places to see," said Mrs. Robertson flipping through the contents of another file in her phone.

"All right Ryan... That would be the next place that I go to and you young man will be a dutiful nephew who will accompany his aunt."

"Aunty... but," he started to try thinking of a way to excuse himself.

"Be a dutiful nephew..." she pretended to chide him and then in a serious tone continued,

"You need some relaxation and diversion too Ryan... All work and no play will make Ryan a dull doctor."

"All right aunty... I will b e a dutiful nephew who accompanies his Aunt."

"And Geetha please do come along too. It will be a mini break for you too. Please bring along your parents too or any of your friends. "

"Oh no, Mrs. Robertson, I am afraid it may not be possible..."

But Mrs. Robertson persisted and Geetha found herself saying that she would check with her parents.

The waiter soon came to take their drink orders.

"Pineapple juice will be good for you Aunty," suggested Ryan.

"Oh alright." smiled the Aunt. She was happy to see her

nephew looking relaxed and caring just like the good old days.

"And what will you have Ms. Geethanjali?" he turned towards her.

"Mosambi juice with no water and ice, " she answered.

"Wow...that's my choice too," he smiled.

"Mosambi?" quizzed Mrs. Robertson

"Orange juice, aunty," smiled Ryan.

"Oh," nodded Mrs. Robertson, "So how was your trip to Delhi?"

"The seminar was excellent. My paper was appreciated and it has been taken up for further review."

"Well so you just spent all your time on ...," began the fond Aunt.

And the fond nephew understood what she was about to protest.

"Well as a matter of fact I did go to Agra nearby for a sightseeing visit as you had suggested," he smiled   .

"Oh good, where are the pictures. I cannot wait to see them." cried the Aunt excitedly.

The doctor smiled sheepishly. A couple of minutes of silence passed.

"So, let me guess...you forgot to take pictures?" volunteered the Aunt.

"Actually...it's not the pictures. I took loads of them," he paused, "It's the camera."

"You forgot the camera! It was a brand new DSLR Ryan!

"Aunty...I know!"

"How many things that you keep forgetting Ryan?"

"Aunty," he started to say and then stopped abruptly. He

turned in the direction of the pianist. His Aunt followed his gaze and then she heard it too.... the opening exquisite notes of Fur Eliste were being played. But obviously not so exquisite to her nephew's ears.

Wasn't that the song that Amanda had walked down the aisle to?

"Oh no," she thought. Has he not changed even a bit? Could he rather not forget that episode in his life? Has he got to be so sensitive of everything that was associated with his brief failed marriage with Amanda. The genial young man's face reddened.

"I need to go," he murmured and almost jumped out of his seat and shot out through the door as the two ladies watched him go.

"He must have received an emergency page," murmured the Aunt to Geetha trying to excuse her nephew's actions.

And just then the waiter emerged with the juices they had ordered.

"Thank You," said Mrs. Robertson feeling really thankful for the diversion and regaining her composure a bit.

Geetha took her juice too thankfully. She had her own realization too to process then as she saw him turn and vanish through the door. Oh yes.. Dr. Ryan Richardson indeed. It was Mr Stranger indeed.

10

FIRE ON THE MOUNTAIN

THE TEAM meeting ended on a dismal note. Geethanjali walked out thoughtfully.

"This is the regular grind. I have an interview lined up anyways later this week," she heard a colleague whisper.

Just when she was getting settled in her new job, this news had to come, she worried.

Slowly she walked to her seat mechanically and sat down absent mindedly.

"Is something troubling you Ms. Geethanjali?" asked a voice kindly.

"Is the state of the financial health of our hospital really so bleak?" she blurted out.

"Well unfortunately I only can diagnose the hospital patients' health issues, not qualified to diagnose the financial health of our hospital itself," replied the voice jokingly.

The answer jolted Geetha out of her thoughts and she looked up aghast to see a genial Dr. Ryan Richardson sitting in front of her.

"Oh, I am sorry ...I did not realize. I was thinking of just the health industry in general," she tried to manage.

"Well do not bother Ms. Geethanjali. It is a known fact here. In fact, they have just completely closed down the Kerala branch. I was actually working there and I have just been recently transferred here to Chennai."

"Oh...is that why I have hardly seen you here before?"

"Yes," answered Dr. Ryan. And then he questioned, "So, why are we suddenly remodeling the downstairs floor if our situation has not improved."

"Oh well ...that is the general waiting area for our patients. We just thought that it will make a more pleasing experience for them," she answered hoping feverishly that his forgetfulness would kick in and he would drop this topic.

He smiled slowly, "Well an attractive package surely matters. But what finally matters is the contents within ..."

Geethanjali could not help agreeing that he had a point there.

"So, what brings you here Dr. Ryan? Is there something or someone that you are looking for in the admin department. They had left for lunch directly from the meeting."

"Oh no, Ms. Geethanjali ...," he hesitated for a moment.

"Hope aunty is doing well," she inquired wondering at his hesitation.

"Of course. It's just that her BP shoots up a little on and off especially when she worries about problems. And the beauty of it is that, she never worries about her problems. It's the problems of those around her that troubles her."

"Well you have a wonderful aunt," smiled Geetha. Just like my aunt Shyamala she thought.

"I understand that aunty has earlier shared many details on Sathish, her friend's nephew with you."

"Yes ...,"

"It's just that aunty has suddenly come up with the brain-wave as to how to try and help Sathish... She was wondering if we could take him to an orphanage and he gets to see how life is there versus his life.. then it may give him an opportunity to really count his blessings."

"Yes, that sounds a good idea," Geethanjali nodded wondering who "we" meant in this idea.

"Aunty actually has been sponsoring many children at a particular children's orphanage home over here. So, Aunty was thinking we could go there and was hoping if you would like to join me. It would be of help to me too. I hardly know anybody here yet... and not sure how Sathish is going to react," he completed the request hesitantly.

Geetha slowly nodded her head. She was not sure how she would be able to help Dr. Ryan trying to help out Sathish. But she sure would accompany them.

"That's excellent. Okay, if you could come here to the hospital on Sunday morning around 10 o'clock we could all go together from here.... Or would 10 o'clock in the morning be too early for you?"

"It sounds fine. I can come in earlier too if you would prefer."

"Perfect. That's settled then. Anything before 10 o'clock

on Sunday may actually be too early for me."

"All right Ms. Geethanjali, we will meet you here next Sunday 10 o'clock sharp! Thank You!" he nodded and got up.

"Sure, Dr. Ryan."

And then he paused hesitantly once again, "Actually, the first thing I wanted to say today was that I am sorry about the other day..."

"Oh, not at all," Geetha mumbled surprised at the young doctor's apology.

He looked so genuinely apologetic, such a stark contrast to the deep red angry young man who dashed out of the hotel. Surely, he must be at least 50 percent nice as his Aunt she thought.

"Please do not bother. Your Aunt also said that you must have probably forgotten an appointment...,"

She found herself further rambling, " Maybe you should take an Omega 3 supplement ...I heard it helps with forgetfulness.."

And then she stopped abruptly. Oh gosh, was she sounding cheeky. But good, he appeared to have missed hearing it. He had a lost thoughtful look.

Yes, Dr. Ryan had hardly heard her prescription. He was lost deep in thought. Forgetfulness...how wonderful it would be if I could just use it to forget what I really need to forget.

And then he slowly became aware of Ms. Geethanjali fervently signaling and shouting words at him.

"It's time to show your dashing powers again Dr. Ryan. Run."

"What?" he asked incredulously.

And then he heard those alarms go out loud and clear incessantly. It was the fire drill in progress.

"Fire on the mountain. Run, run, run." laughed Ms. Geethanjali.

"Fire on the mountain. Run, run, run." he laughed too.

11

THE GIFT OF LIFE

HUES OF blue, orange and yellow appeared to dance as the little girl flourished yet another stroke on her creation. And then as the grand finishing touch, she pulled out some yellow powder and mixed it with the binding material and outlined the edges of the sun's rays to give it a glorious radiance. She turned back and smiled at her three newfound admirers.

"Lovely!" appreciated Geetha.

"Do you like to paint landscapes?" questioned Sathish to the little artist.

"I like to paint sunrises …," answered Kavita a girl of around 11 years.

"Any particular reason?" continued Sathish.

"Many reasons…," Kavita began to answer as Dr. Ryan

joined them.

"To me, the sunrise is the start of the day... The start of very many possibilities of that day... Another start for fulfilling the hopes from the previous day..."

The earnest, thoughtful, innocent response of the little girl took the three adult visitors by surprise.

Such profound thoughts from a little girl who was barely 12 years. Something began to stir within Sathish.

"So, do you want to become an artist?" he continued.

"Not really...," she surprised them yet again.

"There are so many things to do. I would love to be a lawyer. Or maybe be an auditor. Or maybe, be involved with organic farming... There's a long way to go. I have not set my heart on any specific thing yet. Depending on the circumstances at the time I finish my high school I will evaluate my options then..."

"Hey what was the yellow powder that you used?" asked Sathish.

"It's turmeric," answered the little girl.

The trio moved to look over the creations of the remaining children.

"Hey look! What is that child trying to show? It looks so fascinating. Is that a charioteer?" asked Ryan.

"Oh, that's the very famous battle scene from our epic Mahabaratha of Lord Krishna imparting his advice and teachings to Arjuna."

"Oh...," Ryan noted. Before he could question further, a friendly voice greeted them.

"Good afternoon Dr. Ryan, Ms. Geethanjali and Mr. Sathish..."

The trio turned to see the warden of the orphanage Mrs. Revathi Shanmugam walking towards them.

"Good afternoon Ma'am,"

"Oh Mam ... You seem to be raising such little pearls of wisdom over here... But how is this possible? Such confident but pragmatic little children?" questioned Dr. Ryan.

"Arithu arithu Manideerai Pirathal Arithu," the lady broke out into a song to the surprise of all.

"You surely must have heard of that song Ms. Geethanjali? The song sung by our grand old lady -Avaiyaar[12]!"

"Yes...," nodded Geethanjali.

"We inculcate these words and meaning into the minds of our little children over here Dr. Ryan. It simply means ...Unique indeed it is! Unique indeed it is that we are born as a human being!" she translated.

She continued to expound,

"It is the biggest gift from God that we are all born as human beings. He gave us this life for a reason. We need to make the most of this gift. In this game of life, all of us have actually won one half of the game already by being qualified to have been born as a human being. Staying in and winning the remainder of this game solely depends on our subsequent actions in the playground of life. We are not dependent and should not make ourselves dependent on others' actions towards us. Obstacles and setbacks will be there aplenty. But we need to only focus, develop, polish and apply our strengths to overcome any obstacles in our path and keep playing the game... Oh I can go on and on...,"

---

12   Avaiyaar-title of a renowned female tamil poet
-related song was apparently sung in the 12th century BC

Dr. Ryan and Geethanjali both stole a look towards Sathish. Yes, he had absorbed those words and was realizing the folly of his earlier actions. Varied thoughts were rushing through his mind.

"I have loving parents. I already have someone loving in my life. Why did I ever think of throwing away my life for the sake of someone else? What a fool I was? I have been blessed in so many ways and I chose to throw away all of them for one foolish failure or disappointment in life??????????"

"Not any longer!" he resolved himself and looked up to hear the warden continuing

"It's just those principles of counting the blessings and to rely on ourselves on multiplying those blessings is what keeps us and those children cruising through life. And of course, we happen to know that there are people out there like all of you who care for us and will give us the lending hand..."

"Aunty, all the chairs have been arranged," came up a little girl to the warden.

"Please come on in... The children have organized a little something special for all of you'll to enjoy too..."

12

I'M GOING TO WIN

AN HOUR later, Dr. Ryan, Sathish and Geethanjali went outside to the garden where a few other donors and volunteers were also gathered with the children. It was the final game for that day. Chairs were arranged in a circle. They had earlier finished a game of passing the parcel and all three of them had lost out miserably in the initial rounds itself.

"What is this game now?" Dr. Ryan looked curiously.

"Oh, it's musical chairs!" answered Sathish, "And this was always a part of the games which my parents used to organize for my birthday parties."

"Well I feel like a little boy," joked Ryan.

Me, a little girl, thought Geethanjali.

They were assigned the chairs by the children and

Geethanjali found herself seated by Dr. Ryan.

"So how do you feel our luck will turn out now?" whispered Dr. Ryan to Geethanjali.

Before she could answer, Sathish from behind answered, "Not luck sir. It all depends on our skills."

Ryan and Geethanjali could not help smiling at Sathish's new found resolve and behavior.

And then the music started. Everyone got up and ran around and around the chairs. The music stopped.

A man in blue shirt was the first to leave the game.

"Wow, we are still there," commented Dr. Ryan. Geethanjali smiled in agreement.

"Yes!" said Sathish and gave Ryan the high five. The music resumed and then stopped. The three of them found themselves still in the game. Sathish gave Ryan another high five.

Wow, she thought, those two were certainly in high spirits. Well, she herself felt like a little girl wanting to give a high five too. The game moved on. Slowly, one by one, the other players dropped out. And the three of them found themselves in the final three.

"This is cool!" shouted Sathish, "One of us is going to win!"

The music did not start. The new highlight of the game was that the children were rather going to sing. Everyone cheered. The children started to sing. Sathish tried to carefully be near one of the chairs. Ryan too tried to carefully be near one of those chairs. And Geetha, not to be left behind was also eyeing the chairs and mapping the distance. And then the children stopped singing. Ryan found the chair and sat down in it immediately. He turned and saw Geetha sitting in another chair. Sathish walked away showing the thumbs-up sign to them. Ryan and Geetha exchanged triumphant smiles.

"I'm going to win, Geetha!"

"I'm going to win, Ryan!"

He was no longer Dr. Ryan. She was no longer Ms. Geethanjali or Ms.Vasudevan.

The little childlike spirit in them was in full play.

The children started singing again. It was the final round. The cheering reached a crescendo.

"Come on Ryan Anna"

"Come on Geetha Akka"

Ryan and Geetha ran around and around the one chair. And then the children stopped singing.

Geetha found herself behind the back of the chair. But Ryan had not sat down yet on the chair. Everyone cheered Ryan on, expecting him to wrap up the game. But no, he still continued to stand.

"Why?" she asked,

"Ladies first," he smiled at her.

"Oh, no thanks..." she mumbled taken aback by that sweet gesture.

And then to their surprise, the children started singing again.

"One more round to determine the true winner," Ryan joked.

And then the children's voice faded to a stop. This time Ryan found himself far away behind the chair and Geetha was standing right beside it. But she did not sit.

"Go on!" he egged her on.

"Nopes Mr. Ryan...Ladies know to return a good deed

too..."

And then as their tug of war of sportsmanship continued, an announcement was sounded by the warden Mrs. Revathi Shanmugam.

And the winners of the musical chairs is Ms. Geethanjali Vasudevan and Dr. Ryan Richardson.

"Wow!" exclaimed both Ryan and Geetha and they could not help laughing at each other.

13

NEXT INNINGS

"Many thanks to Dr. Ryan for offering to come in on the weekends and be a consulting doctor for us." warmly thanked Mrs. Revathi Shanmugam.

"Oh.. not at all Mam... It's the least I could do."

"And Mam," started Sathish, "I would love to volunteer some time weekly too to take some math or science classes for the children."

"Of course, certainly... the children would enjoy it ... Thank you!"

"God bless all of you!"

Bidding their farewell to the children and Mrs. Revathi Shanmugam and the other acquaintances gained in the orphanage, the happy trio trooped out of the garden and made their way to leave.

And then a picture in the hallway caught Ryan's eyes and he stopped them all abruptly.

"Isn't that the same picture representation of what the children had drawn. That scene which you mentioned was from the epic?" he quizzed.

"Well yes, you are truly fascinated by it, Ryan" teased Geetha.

"Yes... Look at those words written above it!"

"Well those were the golden words said by Lord Krishna to Arjuna or to the world at large."

"Whatever happens or has happened is for the good.

Whatever is happening now is also happening well.

And whatever will happen will also happen well....,"

she translated and then paused as the full intensity of the words struck her.

Not only did it strike her, but it had equally enlightened the men.

"Yes, whatever is happening now is happening well...," murmured Ryan.

"So, whatever will happen in future will also happen well?" said Geetha slowly.

"Yes, what will happen in future will also happen well!" said Sathish.

It was as if they had been given the final cleanse of all the painful memories and baggage that were weighing them down and were now finally free to live and experience all the new possibilities and blessings that life was waiting to bestow on them. They were ready to get on with their innings in the grand playground of life.

14

JUST ANOTHER DAY

A CONTENTED SMILE tainted with a slight amount of pride enveloped Mrs. Akila Vasudevan's face as she slowly turned over the pages of her younger daughter Renuka's engagement album. She relived the moments of her daughter's engagement that were captured in the pictures.

"So, what do you think Akka of the bridegroom's family?" asked Mrs. Akila Vasudevan to her elder sister Mrs. Shyamala Sundaram as the aunt slowly browsed through the pictures of the engagement album.

"They do look like really nice people," confirmed the Aunt, Mrs. Shyamala Sundaram.

"At last we have had a happy event take place in the family .... after Geetha's divorce," mused the mother.

And just then trooped in Geethanjali, armed with shopping

bags of vegetables,

"Hello Aunty!" greeted the niece warmly.

"Hello Geetha...Oh you went shopping at this time of the day? Is it not too hot?"

"True, aunty. But this is the time when the vegetable loads from Ooty arrive and I wanted to get to them as fresh as possible. And, I'm able to do this only on my holidays." chatted Geetha.

She began sorting out the produce purchased and carried over one bag to the kitchen.

The aunt continued to browse through the album.

"Lots of new faces," she commented.

"Yes, they are the boy's relatives and friends."

"Akila, where is Geetha in all these pictures? I still have not seen a picture of her!"

"Oh... she...," fumbled Mrs. Akila in a search for words, "She had a meeting at work that day...,"

"On a Sunday," thought Mrs. Shyamala Sundaram and then the truth hit her head. She being a widow was not generally a welcome addition to any auspicious events. Did the same fate have to befall this young lovely niece of hers? And then before she could worry further, a cheery voice interrupted her thoughts,

"Oh yes Aunty, I'm a very busy person nowadays. ... Did you not know, I have been promoted as the managing director of the hospital...,"

"Oh...," noted a confused Mrs. Shyamala trying to figure out her niece's joke.

And Geetha, as if she had read her aunt's mind continued, " But, not to worry, Aunty. The wedding is the bigger occasion and we will certainly make our presence felt in the wedding ...will we not Aunty?"

"Ah..yes...," nodded the Aunt scanning her niece's face with wonder.

The joviality in her words matched her countenance. No feelings of resentment or self-pity were masked there. There was a genuine air of cheerfulness and confidence in her eyes and face as she tried to avoid any embarrassing moments for her mother.

"Her going to work and seeing the outside world has been the panacea for her worries...," thought the aunt happily.

"Well aunty... so are you ready and set for next week?"

"Hmmm..." paused the Aunt as she tried to re-switch her thoughts and absorb Geetha's next cheerful question.

"Our trip, Aunty? To Mahabalipuram? Have you forgotten it?" chided Geethanjali.

"Oh yes... I am," smiled back the aunt.

15

CINDERELLA...OF COURSE NOT...

"How are you feeling now aunty?" asked a concerned Ryan as his Aunt Mrs. Robertson applied the pain reliever balm to her forehead. She then passed on the balm to Geetha's aunt asking her to apply it for her aching joints too.

"Try it, Mrs Shyamala. It does seem to be good. And it should work for all pains."

Geethanjali looked at both the ladies with concern. The travel had been a bit tedious. Hopefully, they would soon feel all right.

"It's better now Ryan, but I still need a short rest... There's no point in you also waiting for me here in this room and wasting your time."

"Oh Aunty! we all came here only for your sake, since you were the one who wished to see this place."

"We will be there after lunch and a short rest," persisted Mrs. Robertson.

"After lunch? That will easily be another couple of hours?"

"We are old... my young man...," sighed Mrs. Robertson.

"Oh my gosh...please stop these old-age excuses. It pains me that as a doctor, I'm hardly able to get you to heed my advice. In addition, I've also completed a few courses on Siddha medicine over here, which gives us so many tools in enabling man to live a life healthy and free of all issues. But again, I am unable to get you to follow my diet, protocol etc."

"Oh, young man.... I beg your pardon... I'm not complaining that I'm old... I am just a young toddler needing an afternoon nap..."

"Aunty!"

"Now you stop being a doctor and listen to your aunt and go and see this place as a curious tourist..."

"All right aunty. You win again," shrugged Ryan.

"You carry on too ...Geetha," advised both the ladies. Ryan turned towards Geethanjali.

And her phone just then chose to ring :

"Ulathil nalla ullam ...."

"I will join you downstairs," she nodded as she picked the phone to answer the call.

"Do not forgot the camera, Ryan," reminded his aunt playfully as he picked up his backpack and strode out through the door.

Geetha finished her call and made her way down the stairs feeling a bit uneasy. She and Ryan were good acquaintances and may be a bit more now...good colleagues... but surely not the best of friends to go gallivanting down the shores of

Mahabalipuram. It was most unfortunate of his aunt to get an attack of migraine now.

"Oh, where am I to now find him," she thought with further dismay as she could not see him at the reception hall lobby.

"Mam," a hotel attendant stepped forward, "The gentleman who came with your group asked us to let you know that he will be waiting in the beach. In fact, he's just over there...," he pointed out.

"Thank you," answered Geetha, "Oh you have a direct access to the beach. It's so close by." she was surprised.

"Yes ma'am, that's one of the highlights of our hotel.

"Hmmm... today is a Sunday. But there's hardly anyone around," she couldn't help commenting.

There were probably just a handful of youngsters who were possibly college students swimming in the beach.

"Well ma'am, the entire city is at the IPL 20/20 cricket match finals."

"Oh yes..." She understood and could not help smiling at the people's fascination for the game.

"All right ... Thanks," she politely answered and exited the hotel door.

As she stepped out, the pleasant sea breeze caressed her face. She looked up into the open skies and the blue expanse and some distant childhood memories of her last visit to Mamallapuram woke up within her. She had hopped like a bunny rabbit then. She had flitted like a butterfly then. She had eagerly scoured the beach for sea shells and every find had been a prized treasure.

Her eyes now fell upon a sea shell, but she resisted picking it up. She liked the breeze. One part of her wanted to hop over again. The beach appeared pretty deserted and nobody would notice if she indeed did choose to hop. But another part of her dissuaded her, chiding that there was no bringing back the carefree days of yesteryears.

And then her thoughts froze. Her knuckles froze too for a moment. She frantically tried to assimilate what she was seeing and what she could possibly do. Oh my God! that receding, waving hand in the water was a cry for help.

She could possibly not have time to go to the hotel back to fetch help. With trembling hands, she called up the Hotel front desk. But nobody answered her call. And then she caught sight of Ryan. Ryan was relatively closer to those folks. He could surely help.

And then she took off like a baton relay player to pass on the baton to Ryan.

"Ryan look to your left ...there is someone drowning!" she shouted.

"HELP!" she continued to shout and ran forward towards the group of youngsters and Ryan. But they hardly seemed to turn around. Ryan was there too appearing to just talk on his phone.

"Ryan...Help! that man is drowning!" she continued to yell at the top of her voice as she neared him.

But he did not acknowledge having heard her. He continued to be engaged on the phone.

Whatever is he doing? Can't he hear my cries? Why can't he put down his damn phone and be aware of what's going around she panicked with anger and helplessness but kept running.

"Ryan look to your left ...there is someone drowning," she

continued to shout as she sprinted towards him breathlessly.

And then as she neared, he suddenly turned towards her with a smile.

"Hold on ...hold on...relax, take a deep breath and see."

She frowned wondering whatever he was talking about now, but she followed the direction of his gaze.

"All's well now, It's under control."

Geetha could not believe her eyes. She looked in amazement as she watched the coastguard security walk away with the rescued young man and a group of college students.

"See that's the coastguard. They have rescued him."

And she was even more amazed when few of those boys paused and ran towards Ryan shouting, "Thanks again sir!"

"What happened?" she blurted

"I had contacted the coastguard."

"You had their phone numbers?" she blurted out again in surprise

"Oh, I had just got them at the reception when I had stopped by, before coming here. Generally, I collect all the needed emergency contact numbers etc when I am travelling to a new place."

"Oh..," she nodded in amazement

And then with a twinkle he added ...

"I guess your blood was boiling when you just saw me engaged on the phone,"

"Well not exactly...no not at all," she muttered trying to pretend otherwise as she sheepishly looked down and was relieved when he himself changed the topic.

"So where do we go now ...while we wait for our aunts to join us too.?" He pulled out his collections of maps and shared it with Geethanjali.

"Geetha...you surely must have been here many times .... suggest the best place," he asked her.

"Well I have been here ...but I was pretty young then.... I remember hopping around...I remember running around...I remember collecting a lot of sea shells ...but I do not remember anything further ...everything looks new," she mused as her eyes caught a sculpture a little distance away.

"Seashells ...," mused Ryan with another twinkle.

"Actually, there is a sea shell museum. Probably you will like to go there then."

"Sea shell museum ...?" wondered Geetha. It sounded new to her ears. She looked at the place Ryan was referring to in the brochure.

"Oh, this is a new museum built here ...," she read.

And then she pointed out another spot in the map.

"Arjuna's Penance...how about that if you are interested in stone sculptures? Your aunt was particular only about seeing the shore temple. She will not surely have the stamina to go visiting Arjuna's penance,"

"Sounds like a good plan...To Arjuna's Penance," agreed Ryan.

"We need to walk quite a bit, but this seems to be the quickest one," he traced the route they needed to take,

Geethanjali nodded and she put out her foot to start moving.

"Ouch...!" she let out a cry. "My feet ...," she cried out in pain and plopped down on the sand.

"May I check?" he asked and as she nodded, he gently held her foot and examined it.

"It's just some blisters coming up. Walking in the hot sand without sandals has aggravated it. So where are your sandals?"

"Oh ...?" Geetha looked down with surprise. Where were her sandals?

She looked ahead and noticed them strewn a few meters away. "Oh, over there... It must've slipped out when I was running towards you folks. I didn't realize the pain all this time but it's terrible now....," she grimaced.

"Just apply this ointment for now," he said producing a small tube from his backpack. "And in the night when you get back home you can probably apply some glycerin and rosewater. That should suffice."

Geetha gratefully took the ointment from him and began applying it liberally.

"Thanks Dr. Ryan! It feels truly better," saying she looked up and was surprised to not see him standing there.

And then for the second time that day her thoughts froze. She stared with dismay and surprise as she saw him approaching her carrying her sandals back towards her.

"Here ma'am," he handed them to a dumbfounded Geetha.

Did she feel like Cinderella? Surely not...but something surely tugged inside somewhere deep within her.

16

THANK YOU

THE TWO visitors were hardly prepared for what greeted them. As the guide hurled facts on the brilliance of the mid-7th century masterpiece, "Wow....!" was the sole word that escaped from Ryan's mouth.

The guide enjoyed Ryan's mesmerized appreciative looks and re-emphasized and repeated his last statement, "Yes sir... It is indeed carved out of just one stone."

"Indubitably!"

Ryan turned towards Geetha who was also soaking in the artisanship of the carvings on the stone.

"I wonder what it would have taken for the king to visualize such an end state and what did it take for the people in that era to have made all this possible. It's a celebration of dreams, sacrifices, resourcefulness, toil and execution."

Geetha nodded in agreement, "They have portrayed the severe austerities which the Prince Arjuna had to undertake to win the Kurukshetra war. But I wonder what the King and the subjects underwent to create such a great masterpiece to inspire and enthrall all the future generations over the centuries"

"Arjuna!" thought Ryan." Oh, I remember now. Is he the same prince who was represented in the picture we saw the other day in our orphanage visit?"

"That's right." Geetha nodded.

"Excuse me sir. I will be back in 15 minutes," the guide interrupted them and excused himself.

"All right." nodded Ryan.

"Let's take some pictures now, Geetha. Auntie wanted a lot of pictures." he smiled.

"Well firstly let me take your picture. Stand over there." He directed her to stand against the backdrop of the carving representing Arjuna's one legged penance.

Geetha too followed his orders.

"Smile Geetha. It's your favorite character in the epic." He encouraged her to smile for the picture.

Geetha broke out in an amused smile. "Whatever makes you think he is my favorite character?" she continued to smile.

"Thought he was the main character in the epic. So, presumed he must be your favorite character. Is he not?" answered Ryan as he handed over her camera back to her.

"No, he is not. My favorite character will always be only Karna."

"Oh, that's a new name... but wait a minute...I have actually heard that name too. Is it not the same name which is on your ring tone song?."

Geetha was taken aback for a second. She could not help wondering that he had noted the ring tone of her phone. As if reading the question on the mind, he himself answered,

"Actually, the voice on that song is so very rich.... And the music sounds so poignant."

"Yes... That's a song from the film on the life of Karna .... "

"Alright Geetha...I will stand over here and you can take my picture now. Please ensure all these carvings all the way to the top are captured," he requested as he adjusted the focus on his camera and handed his camera over to her.

"If you ask me about Karna I can go on and on, but I will tell you very briefly," chatted away Geetha as she clicked his shots.

"That song actually walks through his greatness and demise and ending on that same battlefield. For the sake of gratitude, he aligned himself with the King whom Arjuna fought against. He was one of the most charitable persons that ever lived and he sacrificed his hard earned boons of military prowess to honor the requests of his biological mother and thus lost his life. Of course, his glory will always live in the minds of all who hear his story," her enthusiasm slowly dimming as she recalled his tragic ending.

"Are these pictures, fine Ryan?" she asked as she tried to divert herself from the sudden sad thoughts.

"They are fine." answered a subdued Ryan too and then his next question shook her.

"And do you consider yourself too as having lost like Karna?"

He is too deep she thought. Is he now a psychiatrist too, she wondered.

"Oh..." She blushed scrambling for words.

"I just like that song for the music and that rich voice like you mentioned too."

And then she muttered to her surprise," Maybe subconsciously yes...,"

She found herself blurting out as they walked around the stone masterpiece with Ryan clicking pictures from different angles,

"Yes, my father for his gratitude towards a relative of his, arranged my marriage with someone without any careful thought. And I out of blind adoration and faith in my father consented to that marriage though I had no good feelings in that alliance."

"And see where I am now... Failed in this life ...!"

"At least Karna got a nice life and his glory will continue to live forever amongst generations, but who is going to sing my praises as a dutiful daughter?" She tried to find some humor in her plight.

A brief pause ensued and Ryan carefully clicked a few other pictures. He then put away his camera and turned towards her.

"Geetha.. I feel your pain. I'm in no better boat. In fact, I have no one to blame for my failed marriage except for myself. No outside forces forced that marriage on to me.... And still here I am... trying to find solace and get back on course."

"Success in marriage would have been perfect, but come to think of it, we are actually not too bad."

Geetha looked up at him feeling puzzled ....

"It could have been worse. We could have still been tied in that unpleasant toxic relationship. And that would have sucked all the other facets of our life too."

"At least we are now left with hope."

"Hope! " sounded Geetha after him, slowly following his train of thought.

"Yes, hope of a better tomorrow,"

"And Yes just... like those golden words...

Whatever happens or has happened is for the good.

Whatever is happening now is also happening well.

And whatever will happen will also happen well....,"

And at that moment Ryan's phone rang. It was his aunt. The two aunts were feeling much better and were ready to meet them for lunch in the lobby.

"All right, let's make a move back to the hotel. Has our guide not returned yet?" he turned to look around and saw him chatting with a few other people a little distance away.

"Let me ask him to meet us at the Shore temple after an hour," said Ryan and walked away towards the guide.

"Shore temple in the afternoon, Sir?" repeated the guide to Ryan when Ryan informed him of his plan.

"Sir, actually the shore temple will be very magnificent in the rays of the morning sunrise., please at least plan your next visit accordingly. You and your wife would enjoy the splendor of that temple even more."

Ryan was taken aback at his ramble. He hurriedly turned back. Could Geetha have heard these words too? And then he was surprised at what he saw. Whatever was she doing now? Why ever was she standing one-legged? Is her other leg paining now? Certainly not, her face was all smiles – as bright as the sunny skies. Or was she imitating the posture in the carving? And then he smiled amusedly as he understood what the generally pensive and serious Geetha was doing. She was trying to hop around.

"Shall I take a picture?" he shouted in her direction.

"Of course ...Thank You!" she hopped about.

17

AN EXAMINATION

M RS. SUNDARAM awaited her turn in a resigned lack-luster manner for the 12 o'clock noon appointment. An anxious Geethanjali watched her aunt's face with consternation as she was aware of her aunt's wariness of hospitals and medications after many repeated failed treatments.

"Hopefully over here, her experience will be different," Geetha prayed inwardly.

Yes, her aunt had vowed never to set a foot inside a hospital as far as possible, but here she was, thanks to the insistent pleas of Dr. Ryan and his aunt during the Mahabalipuram trip that she needed to come and see Dr. Ryan for a consultation and examine his treatment options.

"Geetha, how many more patients are there to be seen, before our turn?" asked the aunt to her niece just as a patient exited out of Dr. Ryan's consultation room.

The clock in the hallway slowly started chiming. 12 o'clock had arrived.

"Wow...a grandfather clock is over here," observed her aunt with surprise.

"Yes aunty, that was a gift during the initial opening of the hospital."

"Well, I wonder how long they are going to make me wait over here," her aunt worried.

"Oh aunty, it's not like the other places you have been to," consoled Geetha.

And hardly had she finished saying those words and hardly had the clock finished sounding the last chime, when the door opened and out came Dr. Ryan himself.

"Mrs. Sundaram, please come in,"

Geetha smiled at her aunt's surprise.

Mrs. Sundaram had earlier resolved never to greet a doctor again, after being tired of her countless greetings and Thank Yous' during the past few years to the numerous doctors who used to hardly even acknowledge them.

But to her pleasant surprise again, she was greeted first by the doctor himself.

"Hello Mrs. Sundaram. Take a seat."

"Good afternoon, Doctor," she found her apprehensions slowly melting.

"So how are you doing Mrs. Sundaram?"

"Not too good doctor. Some days are good and most days are bad. And today is bad," she said pointing to her knees.

"Well then, that is soon going to change then," he continued to smile kindly taking the medical files from Geetha.

"And there are the latest lab reports," the aunt pointed to another folder.

Many moments of silence ensued as Dr. Ryan slowly pored over the files jotting down notes. Many decades may have passed since she had finished her schooling but the elderly lady felt like a little student all over again watching a teacher review her test papers.

"I guess my arthritis is pretty severe. Am I right Doctor?" questioned her aunt anxiously.

"Can you try to make a fist," he asked beginning to physically examine her.

"Would you believe it Doctor, I was a tennis champion at school and college and now I'm reduced to this state," she poured out in despair.

"Wow that's nice... Then you should actually have a lot of fire and fighting spirit ingrained within you," encouraged the doctor kindly.

"I guess so... That's what keeps me going still..," mused her aunt, "But not enough to win over these diseases. I had to give up my painting profession. I can't even hold a slightly big ladle now."

"And now these diseases have become my lifelong buddies," she further continued.

"Oh no Mrs. Sundaram. I would say that they are just some unwanted guests who have overstayed their welcome but who soon need to vacate the premises," he smiled as he wrapped up her physical examination.

"How many hours do you sleep Mrs. Sundaram?"

"It's pretty less doctor. I find it hard to fall asleep or sleep long ...I guess it's the pain too," admitted Mrs. Sundaram.

"All right Geetha, you can have these files back," he handed over the files and began writing on their hospital prescription pad.

"Are they corticosteroids, doctor?" asked Mrs. Sundaram anxiously

"I did read your entire medical history and I'm not going to be giving you those," answered the doctor as he kept writing away.

"Or the other one...imm...immu...," she tried to recall searching for the word and looked up at Geetha.

"Immunosuppressants, Aunty," Geetha helped her with the word.

"We will quieten the immune system differently," the doctor smiled gently looking up at the Aunty and niece.

However, the anxious Mrs. Sundaram tried to peek at what was being written. What were those strange long words? They sure could not even be pronounced. She glanced at her niece trying to catch her eye.

Geetha followed her eyes and rested on those words. For a moment she could not first help admiring how neat the prescription was being written. She had never seen such a legible prescription from a doctor before. She had always been of the view that they wrote in a secret code language which only the pharmacist could decipher. She felt her Aunt's nudge, recalling her back from her thoughts to her aunt's concerns. She again re-read those words.

"Oh, they just appear to be strains of probiotics, Aunty," whispered Geetha back.

"Oh ok," Mrs. Sundaram was momentarily relieved, but again looked anxiously as the young doctor seemed to keep writing and writing away. Again, she felt like the little student now waiting for her teacher to deliver the long, dreaded report card. And then finally the wait was over. Dr. Ryan put down his pen.

The aunt and the niece sat up in attention.

"Zinc..., lots of Vitmain D3.., lots of Omega 3 fatty acids ...,Magnesium ..., Calcium citrate ...B12...," the doctor explained the prescription as Mrs. Sundaram listened in surprise.

"Is that all Doctor?" asked Geetha as Dr. Ryan handed over the prescription to her.

"Actually, I have ordered a few more tests that she needs to take."

"Oh, are these the ones? CRP ...," clarified Geetha beginning to read a section of the prescription.

"Yes, all the ones starting with it ...I need to assess her inflammatory markers in detail and then I will share a complete protocol to be followed and the needed changes in diet and lifestyle too."

"For now, I have also prescribed some physiotherapy exercises for her. We will schedule our physiotherapist to visit her at her place."

"Is there not a painkiller?" wondered Geethanjali.

"Oh...I can bear the pain Gethanjali. I am used to it," interjected her Aunt proudly and also afraid that he might add up some other stronger drug.

"Geetha, take this oil bottle," he said pulling out a tiny bottle from his desk drawer.

"Now immerse the bottle in this cup of hot water to warm it," he further directed, pouring her some boiling hot water from a flask.

"This should suffice. Just, a little. Now apply it on her finger joints and knee joints, so that it is completely absorbed."

"Oh... It's all right Doctor. I can try this at home." murmured Mrs. Sundaram in surprise to see what was happening.

"Is this right?" asked Geetha as she began to massage in the oil.

"A little more pressure and circular motion at the joints,"

"Mrs. Sundararam ... You have a lot of power within you. That's what has helped you put up with the pain all these years. Now you need to harness all your power, to actually get rid of the pain.... everything that is unwanted within. It sure will not be an overnight victory. However, it sure would pave the path to victory."

Mrs. Sundaram felt the warm soothing sensation of the oil and touch near her joints. And at that moment, she did not know if it was indeed the oil or just the concern and optimism of the doctor and her niece, but for a moment she did feel hopeful that the invaders of her health would soon leave her premises. And who knows she may even be able to hold her paint brushes again and she smiled.

18

REGINITE

"Open your mouth nice and wide," said the little doctor and flashed her little torch inside her patient's mouth.

"Dammu ... Do not switch on the torch, the battery will be wasted..," warned another little child.

"Shhhh... Call me Doctor," ordered little Dammu.

But she switched off the flashlight and continued to examine the patient's mouth.

"Aah...," Geetha opened her mouth nice and wide. Geetha and the little children at the orphanage home were playing a pretend game of doctor and patient and Geetha was their giant patient.

"Do you eat a lot of chocolates?"

"Oh...no ...doctor...just occasionally. And I brush my teeth very well."

The doctor put away her flashlight carefully.

"And now for the best part...," smiled the little doctor.

"What's that Doctor?" Geetha asked playfully.

"It's an orthoscope, to see if there are monkeys in your ears,"

"Oh," smiled the pretend patient.

Geetha pretended to squiggle and wiggle as the little doctor looked around the ears

"Any monkeys, doctor?" she giggled.

"Actually, nice and clear."

"Let me see if there are whales bellowing from your lungs,"

"Oh..," smiled Geetha. What will be next? She wondered as the little doctor folded the ends of her paper stethoscope gingerly around her ears.

"Now breathe nice and deep," The little doctor pretended to listen to her patient's breathing.

"Good," declared the little doctor.

"You have just a mild cold. And here's your prescription." She said handing over a piece of paper to Geetha.

"Thank you doctor... Here's your fees,"

"Oh... fees?" said the little doctor puzzled.

"But Dr. Anna[13] does not take fees...," the little doctor spoke slowly and returned her fees.

"It's a free medical camp, aunty." said a bigger child standing in the line of pretend patients.

"And here is your medicine," said the little doctor handing out a piece of stone to Geetha.

"Careful... This is a bottle of yummy pure honey. It will soon turn you from a croaking frog into a singing cuckoo."

---

13   Anna-brother

"Thank you very much doctor," smiled Geetha holding the stone carefully.

"Wait...take this too...," she handed a few pieces of tiny pebbles,

"Keep this handy as a precautionary measure always... whole black peppercorns....helps prevent these issues especially in the cold seasons."

"Oh certainly Doctor...Thanks again," she held it even more carefully remembering that it used to be called black gold once upon a time.

"You're welcome. Take care."

"Next patient please."

Geethanjali carefully pocketed the precious medicine and made her way gingerly to a bigger child seated just a few steps away on the other side of the Banyan tree. The home had become her temple for every Sunday morning visits. Watching and absorbing the banter of the children as they playfully dealt with their situation invigorated her senses and soul. She had assumed the responsibility of doing extra coaching for the children preparing for the board examinations.

Hearing her footsteps, the child looked up from her book with a welcoming smile, "Akka, I'm all done." said Mariam and held up the book to Geetha.

"Wow, perfect!" exclaimed Geetha as she browsed through the solutions.

"You will soon be Ms Pythagoras of your class!" she declared to the beaming Mariam.

"It's all your help Akka!"

"Oh nopes, little Mariam. It is you who is doing the work of studying."

"Let's see what else are the pending topics for this year's mathematics lessons. Differentiation, integration...," she read out and then grimaced, "Lagrange's theorem..."

Oh God...did she have to finally learn this for little Mariam's sake. She clearly remembered avoiding it like a barge pole in her school days. But it looked like, it was not going to give up until she surrendered herself to it. Oh... what was she going to do now, she mused.

"Let's do some science, akka," Mariam interrupted her thoughts picking up a science textbook. "Sure," answered Geetha. Science was not her cup of tea, but she sure could try.

"I have some questions on the topic that I was reading." The little girl stopped flipping at a particular page and pushed across a diagram of a cell body structure and pointing to some parts asked, "What is that, akka?"

"Parts of a cell. Mitochondria, nucleus, nucleolus, cytoplasm....," Geetha read aloud the marked parts.

"It will be the cytoplasm, Mariam," she declared.

"No Akka. I meant those long tubular structures shown within the cytoplasm...!"

Oh gosh. This was turning out to be tough for Geetha.

"Cytoplasm.... Cytoplasm...," She repeated out aloud trying to scan the rest of the contents of the page.

"Those long tubular structures shown within the cytoplasm...." repeated the little girl hoping that it will provide some helpful clues for Geetha's search.

"Cytoskeleton!" a familiar voice to Geetha sounded.

Looking up Geetha was surprised to see a smiling Ryan walking towards them.

She held out the book to him.

"Oh yes... those tube like filament like structures are cyto-skeleton. It helps give the cell that shape...."

The little girl got up excitedly.

"And what is this, Dr Anna?" asked the little girl pointing to a cluster of small brown blob like structures.

Dr Anna...? thought Geetha. Was it Ryan whom little Dammu was emulating a short while ago?

"Those will be the ribosomes," he answered. "They help make new proteins."

"Oh...let me write it down...," But little Mariam then realized that her pencil tip was almost flat.

"Let me sharpen this and be right back," she said and scurried away inside.

And it was now Geetha's turn to question Dr. Ryan.

"Do you do a kind of medical camp here for the children?"

"Yes bingo! How did you guess that?"

"There are your followers," she smiled pointing them towards little Dammu's play party going on in full swing.

"Wow!" laughed Ryan amusedly. "Well I just started out with a kind of medical check visit every Sunday evenings. It's just today that I came by in the morning itself."

"That's so thoughtful Ryan,"

"Oh nopes, Geetha. It's the other way around. It's actually like therapy for me, a kind of retreat for the soul when you're amongst these little ones."

And then little Dhammu came scampering towards them, "Dr. Anna, I have a patient with knee ache. What is this called which we can use for tapping their knees with?"

"Reflex hammer," smiled Ryan.

"Oh yes," remembered the child scurrying away and shouting, "Reflex hammer to test the flippity flappers are strong like that of a penguin."

"I guess it's a treat to be treated by Dr. Ryan,"

"Oh, come on now Geetha. So what do you do here?"

"Well, I'm not doing anything so exciting. Just trying to be a maths pedagogue to the little ones."

"Oh well," smiled Ryan, "You actually have the tough job to do. So, when do you come?"

"On Sunday mornings."

"All right, I will switch my schedule and come along in the mornings. I can do with some brush up of my math skills."

"What!" panicked Geetha for a second before brightening up.

"Sure. The next class is on Lagrange's Theorem." And sure, enough it had him retreating and they both burst out laughing.

"Oh, I guess I will allow the little ones to have that pleasure while I stick to my business."

Sure enough, it was indeed a retreat to reignite their souls

19

SOME PLUMS,SOME CHILLIES..

S HOULD I be really going today? Maybe, I should have excused myself, Geetha kept brooding.

"Please get down here," suddenly announced the auto rickshaw driver bringing the auto to a grinding halt and her thoughts came to a grinding halt too.

"Why did you stop here itself? You need to go straight and turn right."

"No Amma, there is too much traffic. I cannot go further beyond this point."

The traffic was looking horrendous. A truck was trying to turn back in the middle of the tiny road holding the traffic hostage on both sides.

"How am I going to cross in this traffic, why ever did I agree to come?" she wondered.

As she paid the fare, and took in the hustle and bustle of the road she chided herself,

"Now there's no turning back. First look at the traffic. Pay attention to what's happening now."

As honks of various intensity from vehicles big and small filled the air, she managed to somehow walk down the narrow, hardly existent footpath to the junction where she needed to cross the road.

And then she became aware of someone waving a hand at her.

"Oh Ryan," she was surprised to see him and waved back. "I thought his aunt said he was refusing to come. In fact, that's why I could not refuse her shopping request," she mused.

"Step aside. Coming through," suddenly burst a cyclist coming out of nowhere.

"Wow.... All these vehicles big or small are in the same mighty hurry," she sighed.

"How am I to cross now?" She did not have the reckless inclination to go crossing the road amidst the moving traffic like some other folks. She waited and waited and thus it was a whole 15 minutes before she managed to cross over.

"Hello," cried Ryan as she finally made her way.

"Hello," returned Geetha suddenly feeling embarrassed and a little self-conscious at the time she had taken to cross the road.

"Oh no... that was sensible, the traffic was terrible... One needs to be extra careful," volunteered Ryan as if reading her thoughts.

"I would have come over but had received a call from aunty telling me that she was going to be here any moment and asked me to wait here."

"Oh no problem...," she answered doubly surprised at his thoughts. And then her eyes widened with delight as she saw a small cart parked hardly a few yards away. It was brimming with all kinds of fresh colorful fruits.

"Plums," she cried, unable to believe her eyes.

"Yes ma'am.... It is fresh from Kodaikanal, the load came just today morning," replied the fruit vendor further increasing her excitement. "How much do you want Amma?"

"Not now, I will buy when I return in around a couple of hours,"

"Well, it will be sold off by then," saying he turned over to attend to two other new customers who were checking the plums too.

"Buy it Geetha ... They look really fresh and ripe." encouraged Ryan picking up a plum and feeling it.

"Oh yes there is no doubt about it. Kodaikanal plums are super delicious. I'm just wondering how to take it into the shop when we visit the silk palace."

"That's okay. We can hand it over in the baggage counter."

"All right I will take 1 kg now,"

"No maybe 2... oh actually make it 3 ...," she changed her mind again. These were a rare find for her.

"You should probably take a basket," smiled Ryan.

"I actually wish I could,"

Her eyes danced with excitement and glee as she watched the fruit vendor pick and place the plums on the weighing scale.

"Not those. Please pick those on the left corner," pointed out Ryan to the fruit vendor. The fruit vendor smiled and held out the bulky package.

"I will take it," offered Ryan.

"Oh...please do not bother," she cried but he had already taken over the bag and just smiled back.

"Wow, you also know to choose the best plums," smiled a happy Geetha.

"Oh, they were one of my top favorite fruits. My mom used to make amazing ice cream using it."

"Homemade ice cream?"

"Oh yes... She made everything from scratch. And many a Sundays during the summer season, all of us ...me and my sister used to help her with de-pitting those plums, cherries ...,"

She could sense that faraway nostalgic look in his eyes and voice. Just like my childhood days she thought. Helping Amma while she tries to prepare some yummy food for all of us, she thought.

And they both almost sighed at the same time. "Wow ...I miss those days!" they both said in unison and burst out laughing

"Oh, wow... Maybe you should get some plums too,"

"I would love to, but I have quite a bit of fruit at home already. In fact, I have a basket of Alphonso mangoes,"

"Alphonso mangoes," she thought. Just the previous day, she had been surprised to see them in the hospital kitchen.

"Where did you get them? It is so difficult to find them in a shop ."

"Oh, is it?"

"A couple of my old patients had dropped by with it."

"Oh," was the only word which escaped Geetha's mouth.

Her mind was busy piecing together other puzzles. So he was that mystery doctor that had treated all the staff at the hospital a few days back with those delicious mangoes. That gesture from his patients just spoke volumes on the care he must be offering. But, why does he hardly have any repeat visits from them?

And before her thoughts could further figure out that puzzle further, she felt a small folded paper package thrust into her hands.

"Ma'am I cannot give enough change. So, I have given you some chili peppers,"

"Oh, what will I do with so much of chilies," Geetha looked aghast.

"Give me something else. Maybe some more plums,"

"No ma, am ... That would be worth more."

Geetha looked up at Ryan to see his eyes looking very amusedly at her. It seemed to be joking. Plums and green chilies are a nice combo.

Feeling embarrassed she began to tuck the chili package in the outside side compartment of her handbag.

"Maybe you should have refused it, if you did not like it Geetha."

"Well it's just a minor inconvenience. Surely there might be some use for it."

"Oh well...," but before he could continue further, they heard the bright cheery "Hello!"

Ryan's aunt emerged out of the temple exit gates, waving at them. Geetha quickly finished tucking the chili package in the handbag and they both walked to Mrs. Robertson.

"Wow you came Ryan," she gushed.

"Anything for you Aunty," replied the young nephew with a playful charm.

"Oh, of course ..." she smiled and looked at Geetha continuing further,

"Do you know that ever since I came to Chennai, I have been wanting to go here and he has never come. Always finding excuses and putting it away for another weekend... and now we are here in my last weekend of my trip!"

"Oh Aunty...anyways, here I am today ...,"

"Well of course ...," she smiled and looked again at Geetha. And surprised her by whispering in her ears,

"I just told him that you were coming but did not think that he will come so promptly."

The playful banter took Geetha by surprise. Did she hear right? But, before she could react, she heard,

"Here we are!"

The Silk palace loomed tall in front of them. Beautiful , eye-catching fabrics adorned the huge glass window displays. A grand flight of stairs promised to transport them to a land of fine fabrics.

"I can't wait to shop," declared Mrs. Robertson and started to climb up the stairs, picking pace. Ryan smiled amusedly at his Aunt and followed her..

"I hope you have enough place left in your baggage Aunty. I think you had already purchased quite a bit in Tanjore and Madurai."

"I still have space for another 50 pounds."

And Geetha slowly tagged behind them. With trepidation she climbed up the stairs. A sense of uneasiness again got hold of her. This was the same shop, she had felt excited coming in with her mother when she was bought her first silk skirt for her school dance. This was the same shop, she had felt excited coming in with her father when he gifted her a Kanjeevaram[14] silk sari for her college graduation. But those happy memories did not come to her mind then.

Oh no ...why am I here ...was what her mind was crying. And then a playful but kind voice broke her thoughts.

"Come on Geetha, what's up? Are you wanting to get away to go home and eat those plums?"

The troubled train of apprehension came to a stop. Geetha smiled, Wow he is so right ...I did want to get away. But the thought of those plums cheered her up. Amused at his guess she climbed up the stairs with more vigor or at least some pretended vigor. He reached out for her bag of plums and she too gave it away with a tiny murmur, "Thanks,"

Handing it over to the baggage counter, he turned again towards her, "What happened Geetha? Are you not feeling well?"

"Oh no ....just the sun was probably making me feel a little too uncomfortable ...," she murmured avoiding his direct look.

"Would you like to drink some water?" he asked kindly.

"Oh, maybe I should ...," she continued to mumble and pulled out her small water bottle from her hand bag and took some sips again to avoid his gaze.

"I am fine,"

"Wow you have water too in your bag. That's smart. For a moment I actually thought, you bit some chilli thinking

14   Kanjeevaram-a type of silk saree made in the Kanchipuram region of Tamil Nadu

it was a plum."

"Oh...," Geetha blushed and looked up at him indignantly and then they both burst out laughing. The train of apprehension had departed from her soul. Hop aboard the Train of the Present moments her inner voice announced.

"Welcome to our shop," greeted the shop attendants with a friendly "Vanakkam!" to all of them.

"What would you like to shop for?"

"Oh my... whatever workmanship is this ....is this meant for a princess?" gasped Mrs. Robertson her eyes falling upon a beautiful saree draped on a mannequin near the man.

"Aunty...please remember what we came for first...," whispered her nephew.

"We would like to see Pashmina shawls," smiled Geetha.

"This way please," they were guided and taken to the woolen fabrics section.

"Please sit down,"

Ryan pulled back the chair and made his Aunt comfortable.

"Sit down Geetha," he pulled out another chair for her.

The shop attendant scurried to fetch yet another chair for Ryan.

It was at that time that an elderly couple seated near them began to get up. They had just finished making their selection. But as the lady began to get up her vision seemed to blur slowly and she groped the chair handle again and the other hand stretched out towards her husband for help.

"My pressure medicine," she mumbled frantically.

"Oh my...I did not bring that bag...!" panicked her husband too and his hands began trembling too.

"Phone for the ambulance!" shouted a shop attendant at

the top of his voice

But before he could shout out the instructions fully, Geetha found her handbag whisked away by Ryan and her package of chilies pulled out from the outside compartment,

"Bite," he ordered to the lady thrusting almost the green chili into the lady's mouth.

She shrieked, but the blurriness slowly blurred away and the color returned to her face.

Ryan checked her pulse and announced that she was normal.

"Thank You!" cried the lady and her husband profusely. A shop attendant provided her with some water too.

"Oh please relax. Take a few deep breaths. Have you felt like this recently? What is your diet like?"

The lady looked down a little sheepishly.

Turning towards her husband he continued, "These need to be discussed with her doctor. Please take care of her closely for the next few days."

"Yes sir, will do,"

"Thank You again! You were a god send for us today," cried her husband and folded his hands in gratitude and led his wife away.

Ryan returned their greetings and gave the immediate diet advice to be followed and finally turned towards the patiently waiting Geetha and his aunt.

"Very Sorry about that," he said pointing to her handbag.

"I'm happy that it helped."

"Nice job, Ryan." smiled his Aunt.

"Never a dull moment with me, right Aunty?"

"Oh gosh...!" The Aunt looked up to see a sparkling,

cheerful, confident and alive young man.

Where did that cheerless, brooding and quiet young recluse of the last two years go away? Was it her dear nephew talking like this? When did this transformation happen? Has he wholly returned to his normal self? She really needed to give this happy news to his mother. Her sister would be so happy.

She took her seat again and excitedly feasted her eyes on the colorful pashmina[15] scarves laid out before her.

"Wow... Look at this embroidery of the peacock. So exquisitely done," But her excitement was lost as soon as she saw the price tag.

"What is today's exchange rate for the dollar?" she asked the shop assistant.

He pointed her to the exchange rates being displayed on a board behind them.

"Well, let me calculate," saying she pulled out her phone and searched for the calculator app.

"Oh Aunty ... if you truly like it, why do you have to think so much ...?"

"Well look at this?" pointed his aunt to the shawl. "Will your uncle be very pleased?"

"Wow, that is quite pricey but guess for the workmanship and quality, it must be worth so much?" smiled Ryan turning towards Geetha for her opinion. And he was surprised to see a very subdued, serious looking Geetha lost in her own world of thoughts apparently. Surely, that shawl was not the subject of her thoughts.

Was she actually offended with him for taking her bag?

---

15   pashmina-a fine type of cashmere wool

"Sorry," he whispered looking at her thoughtful face. But she did not respond. "Sorry," he repeated a little louder. She did not respond still. He cleared his throat and now said, "A chilli for your thoughts,"

"What?" jumped Geetha

"Wow! that power of the chilli is truly amazing," smiled Ryan,

"Actually Ryan, seeing that elderly couple and the way you resolved the problem, triggered some thoughts,"

"What?"

"I was just thinking of the numbers in the survey results I was working on yesterday. Your patients have all given you very positive feedback without exception."

"Oh, that's nice...,"

"But they hardly seem to return more than a couple of follow up times visit with you. Why is that?"

"Obviously."

"What? What is the reason?"

"Well ... guess your team is in an analysis mode. I do not want to take the fun out of it. A little puzzle for you and your team to figure it out."

"Well folks ... I am happy to have seen my nephew in action today and Geetha is obviously on to some work related, fact finding mission. But I'll be happier if we have all my shawls selected."

"Sorry aunty. I thought you were mulling over some calculations."

"I have decided to put it away for the time being."

"Wow... Look at this color... I have never seen a woolen shawl in this color before," cried out Geetha as she picked up an intricately embroidered shawl in a hue of turmeric yellow.

"Oh, it is the same color of your salwar kurta," observed Mrs. Robertson.

"And the same color of your shirt too ... Ryan?? Wherever and whenever did you get this?" wondering at his choice of color. This was something completely new in her nephew. She hardly recalled ever seeing him in any shades of yellow.

"Guess it was little Kavitha's art which drew him towards that color."

"Spot on! You cracked this puzzle so quickly!" smiled Ryan and Geetha grimaced.

"Kavitha?" quizzed his Aunt?

"Oh Mrs. Robertson, it was the little girl in the orphanage home that you had sent us to. She had used so many different hues of yellow to paint the sunsrise...,"

"And Aunty, you should have seen it ...you would have been spellbound ... In fact, it was so inspiring that you would not guess what else that it made me do?"

"So, did you change your entire wardrobe to hues of yellow?" guessed his Aunt playfully.

"Of course, not Aunty ...!"

"Buy a yellow sofa? yellow cushions? yellow drapes? "
"Aunty!!!!!!!!!"

"Oh! I know...a yellow Mustang ...? Oh no...there are no Mustangs in India. Maybe you are gifting your parents a yellow Mustang?"

"Aunty...that's enough of wild guesses ... I will tell ...."

"Might be he has started watching sunrises?" Geetha's voice interrupted the playful Aunt and her nephew.

Mrs. Robertson turned towards Geetha. "Oh, Ryan waking up to see sunrises?"

"His mother should have heard this?" And she burst out laughing.

"Do you remember the sunrise whale watching trip we took you Ryan in Hawaii? Oh of course you will not remember. You were sleeping like junior Rip Van Winkle...during the car ride ... during the boat ride ... and even when the whale sprayed the water on the boat ....,"

"Oh Aunty...little kids need sound sleep ...," he cried indignantly and then stopped being defensive, "It was actually not fair of you folks to book a trip at that time..!"

Turning towards Geetha, an almost school boyish Ryan pretended to complain, "And do you know Geetha...I was the one who wanted to see the whale and instead only the big folks got to see it....,"

"Alright Ryan, maybe I should perhaps fast forward to..."

"Aunty ... please, not any more ... that's more than enough ...I thought you wanted to do some shopping," interrupted Ryan before Mrs. Robertson could regale everyone with another tale on him.

And that did the trick. Mrs. Robertson's attention rested on the beautiful shawls again, and again fell on that yellow shawl which was still in Geetha's hand.

"So was Geetha's guess right?"

"Yes Aunty!"

"So how did you guess that Geetha?"

Geetha just stood quietly looking sheepish.

"Oh my...please do not say that you are also an early bird now?" Ryan looked at Geetha incredulously.

Geetha did not look up, but just smiled and slowly nodded.

"Oh my...I am not sure whether, the both of you just sold me sunrises or that yellow is the new color of the season. Either way, I guess I now need to have the yellow shawl," she smilingly took it from Geetha ...and gave it to the shopkeeper.

"I will take it,"

A huge smile broke out on the shop assistant's face too.

Another, whole two hours later, the jolly trio finally wrapped up the last of the purchases for Mrs. Robertson.

"All the billing is in the ground floor and you can then collect the purchases right there," directed the shopping assistant and led them to the elevators.

Ryan pressed the elevator button for the ground floor.

"Thank you Geetha...! I really loved the Kurtis that you selected. I just can't wait to wear them in the hot Florida summers. It would be so comfy."

"And I have the perfect shawls and scarves for the winter."

"Well Uncle is going to be pretty surprised with the purchases you have made." teased Ryan.

"Oh... he will not complain, when he sees those exquisite silk ties that I have for him."

"Wow ... nice plan,"

"Of course, maybe I splurged a little too much ... and I am having a little misgiving about the yellow shawl. It is so unlike me. Will it suit me?"

"Oh no Mrs. Robertson, I see how you admire vibrant colors. And that specific one was a subdued hue of turmeric. It would look totally classy and a nice pop of color on your winter coat"

Ground floor, the elevator announced

The elevator doors opened. Geetha stepped out smilingly and casually glanced to her left. And then her casual glance deepened. Scores and scores of bright grand sarees lined the shelves.

No, she was not taking in the sarees. They were of no interest to her. They might as well have been empty shelves for all she cared. But those painful memories unfortunately came tumbling out from the corner of wherever it was hidden within her. The layout of that section of the shop was just the same as that one horrendous evening. She could still possibly recall where that pretentious, monstrous lady stood and boomed over the shop assistants as she literally made them empty the shelves to find the least expensive bridal saree of all on the pretext on searching for a better design while Geetha and her parents and the rest of the relatives looked about helplessly and awkwardly. Oh, why ever did she not have the acumen to not voice her concerns to her parents that day? What could she have done differently?

She caught her own reflection in the mirror. It was looking pensive. No there was no more room or iota of time to be wasted on regrets or bitter moments. Whatever that is done is done.

Geetha...remember you are supposed to be on the Train of present moments her inner voice too reminded her.

A figure in yellow came up behind her.

"A chilli, for your thoughts," a gentle voice sounded.

Geetha slowly began to smile ...but controlled her smile and tried to look nonchalant, although her eyes twinkled in that mirror.

"Well guess the chilli pepper has lost it's powers! How

about a plum for your thoughts?" and his eyes twinkled in equal amusement.

She could not control her smile and turned back smiling at him.

"Well, I will go and collect my bag of plums!"

20

THE SCRIBBLED PRESCRIPTION

"Good Morning Mr Anantharaman,"
"Good Morning Geetha,"
"Good Morning Mam."
Mrs Sulokshna looked up and nodded.
"What happened Mam? You do not look so well?"
"Just feeling a little tired. I had to drop my child at school today. And, there was so much of traffic too."
"Oh, wait Geetha, who is this missed call from? Looks like a call from our bank. Let me call them back."
"Oh, they must be calling in to confirm our appointment again."
Mr Anantharaman looked at Geetha amusedly. Was, this the same quiet, grim Geetha who would hardly utter more than a word when asked even a question before?

"You are also early Geetha?"

"Oh yes Mr Anantharaman, we have the appointment with the bank manager at 9 o' clock. I wanted to re-check all the docs before we leave."

"Well, that has been postponed. They said they will call back shortly with the new date and timing," Mrs Sulochana declared putting down the phone.

"Again?" Geetha looked incredulous.

"Am afraid so ...,"

"Why are they treating us like this?"

"I even skipped breakfast at home to come here early."

"Me too Geetha."

"Well let's go to the hospital cafeteria. There should be some hot vadas ready now."

"I will join too. I can have some coffee."

"Maybe I will go later," volunteered Geetha, "If all of us leave at the same time, it may become an issue."

"Oh, come on, it will be quick. We will not be missed. And ... anyways we do not know how long we will have our cafeteria ...? "

"What?"

"We used to have a 24- hour cafeteria, last year at this same time."

"And now we are just down to breakfast and tea and snacks. I guess, closing down the cafeteria will be the next austerity measure proposed to reduce our costs."

"Well, anyways we will not miss it too much. Look, what's coming up in that opposite building."

Mrs Sulochana looked outside the window to see what Mr Anantharamman was pointing too.

They read the sign together. "Grand opening shortly."

"World cuisine at one place,"

"Hey Geetha, come see this."

But Geetha was busy pulling out a bunch of files and logging on to her system.

"Come on Geetha...there's nothing you or us can do to stop this problem. So long as the bank keeps extending the credit, we can keep the show going."

"Hmmm...not a viable solution for long ...," Geetha worried as she followed her colleagues mechanically down the steps and down the corridor and into the cafeteria.

She nonchalantly read the menu on the display board and Geetha's face then broke into a smile as she became aware of a friendly wave. Dr. Ryan was standing there in conversation with his peer Dr Priya, yet he took a moment and waved at her and her friends.

Her two colleagues too waved back in surprise at his friendly gesture towards them.

Dr Priya turned to see who Dr. Ryan was waving at. Geetha's two colleagues again raised their hands and waved at her and then stopped abruptly. But Dr Priya was not going to return the wave. She just casually looked past them, ignoring their presence. And then the two doctors walked away, apparently leaving the cafeteria.

Geetha stifled a smile, sensing her colleagues' thoughts and gave her order and walked to the nearby empty table.

"Well, she is the top doctor here. In fact, she has a thriving consultation in another couple of hospitals too. So, guess, she cannot be bothered by us small fry." Mr Anantharaman murmured as he sat down.

"Oh forget it, Mr Anantharaman we have other things to think about too. I just got the message from the auditor on the new date." interrupted Mrs Sulochana as she joined them.

Her solemn face spelled what they feared. The bank was pushing them around. They were not too interested in meeting with them on their latest working capital loan requirements.

The trio all looked silently at one another. What were they to do?

I guess we need to go with the other banks, although their interest rate is going to be way higher.

"But our existing bank is the one whom we have had a relationship with all these decades and it's surprising that they are pushing us around like this."

"Well Geetha, what else can we expect? We just barely meet all our payments. Guess it's time for the cafeteria to soon go."

"My head is paining. I need a stronger coffee," claimed Mrs Sulochana and got up.

"Yes, a super strong coffee for me too," chimed Mr Anantharaman and got up too.

"Not me...," dismissed Geetha as her mind kept flitting through various options without any breakthrough on how to address their problem.

"May I join?" a voice interrupted from behind.

Geetha looked up and was surprised to see Dr. Ryan.

"Oh yes...," she murmured as he pulled up a chair in her table and sat down with his mug of coffee

"How is your Aunt Mrs. Robertson? " asked Geetha as

she tried to redirect her focus.

"She is much better and looks like she is finally off the jet lag phase."

"Oh..good."

"And you look so dull on a Monday morning. What's up?"

"Well ...." Geetha hesitated as she tried to collect her thoughts if she could discuss the gravity of the problems to a doctor.

"Are you anaemic? I can prescribe you some vitamins...,"

"What?" Geetha looked up indignantly at this absurd question, but then saw the kindness mixed with that playfulness in those blue eyes and checked herself.

"Well, it's not me that is anaemic. I guess it's our hospital, that is actually anaemic,"

"Oh," smiled Ryan as he stirred his coffee.

"And no amount of vitamins is going to help it. And I am afraid it just needs some steroids."

"Steroids? Are you sure?"

"Well I do not know doctor...What would you prescribe doctor?"

"You...need a permanent recovery plan...a breakthrough plan,"

A short silence ensued as Ryan ... slowly stirred his coffee.

"Well you are the one who says ... that whatever happens is always happening for the good,"

"Oh no, please do not give me the credit for that. I am merely an ordinary mortal who is trying to lead a peaceful life by applying that principle."

"Alright, Mr Ordinary Wise mortal...do you think that you can apply that principle in this situation?"

"I believe so, yes. It is an universal principle ... and can be applied universally.".

"How so...? I would have accepted that it's for the good...,if somehow people are growing stronger...but that's not the case...yet there are so many hospitals that are folding over...?"

"Think Geetha....,"

"Well, we are still doing our analysis...those numbers and the data are trying to tell a story...but I am unable to fathom it yet,"

"Well ...maybe it is an opportunity to innovate...an opportunity to delve even deeper and bring out the best in us..... an opportunity to adopt a different strategy...,"

Geetha looked at him steadily without batting an eyelid. No, a light bulb did not flash within her. But his belief and his words sparked that thought that there would be indeed light at the end of the dark tunnel.

And at that moment his pager buzzed and Ryan hurriedly got up.

"All the best Geetha to you and your team.!"

As he walked away, Mr Anatharaman and Mrs Sulochana joined her.

"What did he say Geetha?"

"A scribbled prescription ...how do I interpret it ...how do I find the medicine," she murmured to herself

21

MR AROCKIASWAMY...

GEETHA CLIMBED up the stairs wearily carrying her files. Her mission to the bank was a failed one. It appeared that the request for increase in working capital was not going to be approved. She was surprised to see the empty corridors and empty cabin. Where were her colleagues?

"Oh," she realised with dismay. It was the founder's day celebrations and probably it had already started and she was now late. Trust those bank officials to keep her waiting extra long, just to drive home the fact that they were not welcome customers.

"What am I to do? I was so carried away by the meeting with the bank office, that this escaped my mind," she thought wearily in spirit and body as she made her way to the cafetaria where the prayer and celebration was planned.

She slowly opened the cafetaria door without making a noise. Apparently the prayer services had just been completed. There seemed to be a pause in the meeting as the Managing director had apparently stepped aside to take an urgent phone call.

She looked around for an open spot to go to. And then she found a hand waving at her. It was Dr. Ryan from the very first row.

She hesitated. Oh should she go all the way to the front row, when she was late. But eager to share her woes with a helpful friend, she gingerly made her way to sit down.

Mr Anatharaman, her colleague shot her a questioning look on the outcome as she sat down.

She shook her head apologetically. She turned towards Ryan.

"Where have you been?" he asked.

"Oh our usual story ...the never ending quest for funds," she whispered.

"Oh," was all that he managed to say. She waited for his next question. Surely, he would have some interesting observation, she thought. But no, he was so quiet. She turned towards him once again. And then she noticed a very different looking Ryan. Wow, whatever is that? A faraway dreamy look on Ryan?

"What's up?" she whispered again.

But he hardly seemed to have heard her. He just sat in a dream like state and then she saw it. He was munching a sweet and that apparently was the state for his bliss and contentment and hardly registering what she had said. Mischievously, she waved her hands in front of him.

"Hey our founder is calling you on the stage,"

"What?" The trance was broken, "hey why did you do that?"

"Well, you looked lost in some other world. So whatever are you eating?"

"Geetha, you should have them. They are so delicious. I have never had anything so delicious for a long time. But I forgot it's name."

"Oh show me ... oh they are Paniyarams[16]!"

"Right ... that's the name ... I need to write it down!"

And then silence ensued as all the attendees stopped talking .

The Managing Director of the Hospital, Mr Arockiaswany was just about to make his speech. He cleared his throat. He did not look bright and lively or in a celebratory mood. He looked pensive as he observed the crowd for a brief second. And then he managed a smile slowly. He again cleared his throat.

"My dear members of this hospital family...today is a very special day in our hospital's history. This is the 100th Anniversary of our hospital founder Dr Kamraj. Dr Kamraj was the complete personification of a true humane medical service provider."

"He treated his patients as his brother, as his sister, as his father or grandfather or grandmother or in another words as his own kith and kin. His thoughtful caring attitude was the key to his successful treatments. And the people in turn treated him as their very own son. And this hospital, my folks

---

16   Paniyaram-a sweet made out of predominantly rice batter

was thus their gift to him ....in other words this hospital was built by the people and for the people and of the people. And on this very day, the first stone for the hospital foundation was laid down.

"My grandfather was the fortunate person who gained his friendship since childhood and joined him in the management of the hospital. And today my friends, I stand before you humbly in thanking you for all your services in running this hospital. Every service that you perform here keeps alive his fond wish of caring for the people."

And then he swallowed a lump. Was that noble dream going to end that year? Would the hospital be forced to fold up all it's operations that year? His thoughts blurred. He felt a sharp pain in his chest. And in the next moment, clutching his chest he began to fall down.

22

HIS SMILE IS BACK

"Aunt Robertson showed me today all that she had bought in India..... it was so lovely."

"Oh yes, Mom.... She was joking that she is having a wardrobe makeover."

"And then, we saw all of her pictures with you. We missed you Ryan," her voice weakened.

Ryan's eyes mechanically swept towards the calendar hanging on the wall. It was probably 2 years and 22 days, since he had left home, actually left everything to get away from everything.

But before her son could think further, her cheerful voice returned.

"But I am so happy...I think I am starting to see the real smile back on my son's face."

"Oh mom!"

"Yes, the twinkle seems to be coming back in your eyes."

"Oh mom! Surely you cannot see that in a photograph ... unless my wonderful cousin Polly has been tweaking it in Photoshop!"

"Well ...your Aunt saw it!"

"Aah...you chatter-boxer sisters are back at your act together."

At that moment a knock sounded on the door.

"Allright mom, pass the phone to Dad.

"Oh, he has left for office."

"So early? "

"Oh yes, he is super busy nowadays at work."

The knock again sounded on the door.

"One minute, Mom, please hold,"

"Come in."

The nurse popped her head through the door and announced, "Doctor, there is one gentleman by the name Ramanathan, who says that he is your old patient and would like to see you for a few minutes. And he seems to have brought with him a whole gang of merry old men."

"What? A whole gang of merry old men? Alright, send them in after 2 minutes," he informed the nurse and returned to the phone call

"Alright Mom. I will call back a little later. Got to go. Bye. Take care."

A small knock again sounded on the door and it opened. And indeed yes, the nurse was right.

In trooped a posse of jolly old men, in the midst of whom the familiar face of a beaming old man stood, "Hello Doctor.

How are you?"

"Hello, Mr Ramanathan," recognized Dr. Ryan, "What brings you here? How are you doing?"

"Doctor.... I knew your consulting time is over and would be probably leaving but I was hoping to see you for a few moments. I just had to thank ... you!"

"Guess it's been a year since I last troubled you with my list of ailments...,"

"Today I had attended my college reunion ... our golden jubilee reunion and I did feel feel fit as a fiddle ... I would have never imagined this would have been possible even 10 years ago. It was your compassionate, detailed analysis and tailored treatment which actually made it possible for me to regain my active life."

"Oh yes... Rama seems to be stronger than all of us...," quipped a number of elderly gentlemen.

"Well you should probably book an appointment with Dr. Ryan,"

"I've got my health back. I have got my life back...," he said tearing up, "I just had to thank you in person this day."

After a friendly banter and many more thanks, the visitors slowly trooped out. The door closed behind them.

Maybe it's moments like these that keep me going and probably brought back that lost smile which Mom was joking about mused Ryan, when another knock sounded on the door.

"Hello Dr. Ryan," Dr. Priya breezed in opening the door with a huge smile.

"Hello Dr Priya! What's up?" smiled back Ryan.

"So how is Mr. Arokiyaswamy doing?"

"Oh much better. But he has been advised to stay in the hospital for another week for monitoring."

"Anyways, so what are your plans?"

"My plans? My plans for ...?" Ryan's eyes widened.

"Well, what are your plans after the hospital folds up?"

"After the hospital folds up?" Ryan's eyes widened even further if there was any space left to widen.

"Oh Dr. Ryan ... do not act so surprised ... after this hospital closes up ... surely you heard it loud and clear from Mr. Arokiyaswamy's speech ... that's why the poor man himself is in the hospital bed now."

"Our hospital folding up???? Well ... things maybe looking a little financially weak...but all is not surely lost yet...we still have a name. We still have our patrons....we are a 100 year old institution..."

"Oh Dr. Ryan...," smiled Dr Priya beginning to quip when her phone rang interrupting her talk.

"Oh.. I need to go now ...," she got up seeing the caller id on the phone

"All right, Dr. Ryan...we all want the hospital to get the miracle cure that you are hopeful of....but we need to be practical too ...I will be starting additional consultations in another hospital in Adyar starting next month. I am just waiting to formally inform Mr. Arokiyaswamy when he is back from the nursing home. If you wish, I could recommend you in the other hospital too.... Bye ...," she said and waltzed out of the room.

"Bye Dr Priya,"

"Whew!" sighed Ryan and sat down. His eyes looked at the clock ticking on the wall.

"Maybe I should go home. It's been a long day." he began gathering his papers and stethoscope.

Another knock sounded on the door.

"Oh, could that be Dr Priya again?" he sighed. Surely no patients were coming in now. His consultation hours were over an hour ago.

Again, the knock sounded.

"Come in," he put away the last of the papers in the drawers and shut them down.

"Good Evening, Dr. Ryan." a voice welcome to his ears sounded.

A twinkle lit up his blue eyes and a warm radiant smile lit up his face as he looked up.

"Good Evening Geetha,"

A pensive Geetha armed with many files and some pens was standing before him.

"Sit down Geetha."

"Thanks,"

She pulled the chair, but in the process dropped her pens. Hurriedly she dived for the pens and sat down.

"So, what's up?"

He noticed her tightening her grip on the files as she sat down.

"Oh ...are you busy?"

"Not really. I am done for the day. Dr Priya was just here a few mins ago."

"Oh yes, I saw her in the lobby."

"She was stating that she was going to take up consultation in another hospital too and was asking me if I wanted to also explore that option."

"Oh," Geetha dropped her pens again. And again, she dived for the pens and emerged up.

"Wow ...those are some runaway pens," Ryan smiled

"What's up Geetha? What, did you want to discuss?"

"It's...well ...," she paused searching for words.

"Are you unwell? Maybe I should quickly check you." he teased pulling out his stethoscope back from the drawer.

"Oh no...I am fine, thank you."

"Well drink some water."

"Thank you," she welcomed it.

"I think you have something super important to share. Maybe that's a treasure map," he pointed to the file that she was still holding extra firmly in her hand.

She smiled slowly and slowly sipped the water till the last drop.

"Another glass?" he asked shaking his bottle and finding it almost empty.

"Oh, do not bother. I am good. Thanks. Well ...so are you planning to explore Dr Priya's suggestion?"

"Oh... of course not. You know my policy nowadays...I do not want to imagine the worst, before anything really happens. And anyways, whatever happens is for the good and whatever will happen will also be for the good."

"Oh yes.," Geetha's nervousness vanished and a feverish excitement invaded her face. She placed the files and the pens on the table.

"Wow Geetha...at last, you let go of those files,"

"Oh my...," laughed Geetha.

"Anyways, I heard that your team had got a loan approved from the bank for some extra working capital."

"True, but those funds will again be exhausted in 12 months at the most if we continue to not turnaround."

"I also heard that they were assessing on how the nursing staff could be further reduced."

"Ideally, we would need more of such trained nurses."

"What?" Ryan quizzed trying to sense what Geetha was having up her sleeve.

"I'm talking about taking care of our patients in a way that gives them the assurance of being in safe hands of a caregiver who truly treats their well-being as the utmost priority. They and the caregiver are truly the joint partners in ensuring the optimal foundations of their health."

"Well... That's what we already do?" puzzled Ryan.

"I know that you do it in your own personal style. You do go to the bottom of the symptoms, look at them individually and collectively and give them a comprehensive complete treatment plan."

"Ok ...right...."

"And that's where we need to build a structure around and systematize it, so that our patients are wholly aware of it and appreciative of it and realize and feel the whole advantage of trusting our hospital with their health needs."

Geetha opened out the file and pulled out a chart.

"Ryan.... I want your honest feedback."

Her fingers trembled a bit as she spread out the chart filled with many sticky notes.

"This is a patient experience map...,"

"Oh, so this is indeed a map...I was right"

"Doctor Ryan...," she smiled and her tension slightly eased.

"Hey is this the one you and your team were working, the

other day with our patients?"

"Oh yes...this is the final map after collecting their feedback and pain points and even all our doctors' responses."

"Right...I recall that sticky dots exercise you gave us to assess ...so what became of it...,"

"Well ...taking all those into account, I kind of arrived at this solution. I ran it by my team..but before we go any further ...I was hoping if you could help with your honest feedback...if this is feasible or even worth pursuing...,"

Ryan glanced at the experience map and pulled out the next sheet in the file,

Introducing a new product or service for our patients to sign up called

"My Health Buddy."

23

HEALTH BUDDY

An HOUR later a doubly tensed Geethanjali sat in the managing director's hospital room while a doubly cheerful Dr. Ryan hovered around, reading his medical progress report for probably the umpteenth time.

They were waiting for the nurse to complete handing him over all his medications before he retired for the night.

She looked at the machine to which he was plugged to. That must be the ECG monitor. She tried to look at them to divert her apprehension. But she could not make any sense of them. If any, it only quadrupled her nervous thoughts.

"Oh gosh... why did Ryan have to risk this...why unnecessarily raise Mr. Arokiyaswamy's hopes ...why are we disturbing him before he is fully recovered."

And as if sensing her thoughts, she heard a sudden whisper.

"Do not worry. This is the medicine he really needs."

"Alright...I need to trust him...he is the doctor..," she managed a small nod to Ryan.

The last tablet was given. The nurse turned to leave. Mr. Arokiyaswamy turned towards Geetha and Ryan eagerly.

"Tell me Geetha...what is this Health Buddy device that I am hearing about? Ryan just gave me a brief update ...but left out the details,"

"Sir, the concept is that, a moment the patient walks into our hospital, he or she should be able to sense a unique customized patient care experience and the assurance that our team of caregivers are working partners or buddies with them throughout the entire medical prognosis which translates into them functioning at the optimal levels if not perfect levels."

"Sir, we and our patients will partner together by utilizing technology to have a structured way of tracking the progress of the medical complaint."

"This is our current patient experience map ...We did the feedback survey with our patients and arrived at the key patient pain points.... these are in fact pain points, felt by the patients in general."

She displayed another paper board with many sticky notes on it.

"And this is where our new My Health Buddy device steps in."

"And this is our proposed patient experience map."

Mr. Arokiyaswamy slowly absorbed the contents presented.

Geetha for a fleeting moment looked up at the ECG monitor. The lines appeared to be the same. The numbers on it seemed a little different though. But before she could think further, she became aware of an assuring node on her side.

She turned back to Mr. Arokiyaswamy and continued.

"And Sir, these are the paper prototypes of the screens that the users will experience, if you would like to see them now"

"Oh yes, please."

She handed over another bunch of papers with diagrams and flows.

"All right Geetha, now give me the details of the modules on this application."

"My symptoms- this is the first building block of our structured offering to the patient- it is the module in which the patient's symptoms are recorded by the caregiver assigning a scale of intensity of the symptoms reported by the patient and also as assessed by the caregiver."

"So, we are going to be logging it in this module?"

"Yes, it will initially be the doctor or the nurse who records it."

"But even today, we do it in our patient's case history."

"Yes sir...it is recorded in the first visit ...but not always and it is primarily the main symptoms. Over here we are going to be logging every complaint the patient is experiencing and we will be using this as a benchmark to continuously assess the efficacy of the treatment plan. You will see in the later module, how this all ties together."

"Alright, and how about ...My reports?" quizzed the managing director.

"It's just going to be an one-stop repository of all reports and diagnostics performed on the patient."

"My diagnosis - this module records the diagnosis made by the doctor and it bears the link to the symptoms and the diagnostics."

"My treatment plan-this would be a module where all the treatments prescribed by the doctors are laid out and it is further broken down into various sub-categories such as My Medications, My Physical Theraphy, My Lifestyle Changes etc."

"And then the very important module –My Treatment Progress which has two sub categories.

My medicines Tracker–this is the module wherein patients need to log in the medicines they take for that day. This will be done in a very user-friendly way. There would actually be a calendar and the medicines which the patient was prescribed will pop up. The patient simply needs to do tap across the right medicines. The time of the tap will be the time recorded for the medicine."

"Well this is certainly different. But all this involves a lot of time."

"Yes sir... But this time which we spend is the differentiating factor in ensuring the patient is truly well taken care of and is on the right track for treatment."

"A common general complaint in the medical industry is that there are many instances of unwanted treatments, surgeries, delayed diagnosis and so forth. This will definitely put an end to all these pain points."

"All right Geetha. So, what is this My Symptoms Checker. How is this different from the earlier module – My Symptoms?"

"This will be a menu wherein the previously reported

symptoms will pop up and the patient will choose the intensity every day. The data logged by the patient in the *My medicine tracker* and the *My Symptoms Checker* will be monitored by our nurses. This is the check to ensure patients take their medicines as prescribed and their symptoms are decreasing or responding to the medicines as expected. And if this was not happening, they would bring it to the attention of the care provider and they could revise the treatment plan without further loss of time."

Mr. Arokiyaswamy carefully reviewed the paper prototypes of the patient experience screens and then closed his eyes appearing to think and visualize the impact.

Silence ensued. Geetha's eyes again mechanically went towards the ECG monitor. Well the numbers were again different. She was not going to able to interpret it. She next mechanically looked for Ryan. A thumbs up sign greeted her and she smiled back gratefully.

And then the silence was broken. Mr. Arokiyaswamy cleared his throat. His eyes were open. He sported a big smile.

Were they a GO? Geetha and Ryan both tried to interpret his smile

"Alright Geetha... ...I get the big picture. I love the paper prototypes. It gives me an idea of where we are headed."

"Sir, we have not yet done the user testing."

"Well as a patient ...I love it..,"

"Thanks Sir. "

"From a patient's point of view it consciously implants in their mind that they follow the treatment plan and that we are there all the way monitoring, assessing and supporting them in their quest to get rid of the illness as quick as possible or successfully managing their symptoms in case of chronic illnesses to ensure optimal levels of quality of life." chipped in Ryan.

"And when patients see this kind of caring personalized professionalism from our hospital staff they would gladly sign up for this program. But anyways Geetha as you mentioned, let's do a paper prototype testing of the screens with our patients to ensure they really understand and want it."

"Yes sir,"

"And Dr. Ryan ...,"

"Yes, sir?"

"Can you please do the needful to get this all unplugged." he said pointing to the ECG monitor

"I feel fit as a fiddle. Can you please have me discharged. Guess that translates to a 0 on Geetha's symptom checker...."

Smiles lit up the faces of the trio in the hospital room. Could they keep alive the dreams of the hospital founder?

24

NOT YOUR AMYGDALA

IT WAS a surprisingly quiet afternoon on the sands of the Besant Nagar beach.

Geetha was seated on a lone wooden log and she slowly twirled the straw in the tender coconut round and round distractedly.

"Do you want another one Geetha? I think you finished it quite some time back." asked Ryan.

"Oh ...no thanks Ryan...I am fine...," she said putting it away.

They watched Mr Anantharaman finally finish his call and he walked towards them hurriedly.

"Sorry Geetha and Doctor ...it looks like the auditors have asked for another piece of info and I need to get back to the hospital. Please carry on without me."

"Alright Mr Anatharaman, no issues, we will take care of it and will update all," Ryan answered, turning towards a seemingly distraught Geethanjali.

"Whatever happened now?" he asked her as he saw Mr Anantharaman's figure recede.

Geetha just shook her head.

"Enjoy this breeze, Geetha. Take off your slippers," he continued.

"Things are happening too fast. Not sure what made me say all these grand theories. With this all really work?"

"Well, end-user testing of the paper prototypes were a huge success. All our staff are behind it. Everything will be just fine."

"Oh Ryan ... I'm getting cold feet,"

"And that's why I told you to remove your slippers!"

"Very funny... Nice prescription..." she smiled realizing the joke.

"Actually, laughter is the best medicine,"

"Oh my...!" She pretended to act in despair, "Is this the best medicine that Dr. Ryan can prescribe?"

"All right ... Ms. Geethanjali... You need to use your prefrontal cortex and not your amygdala,"

"What?"

"Well you wanted to hear some fancy medical jargon?"

"Thank you doctor," smiled Geethanjali, "I'm impressed," she said as she opened the phone to google the terms.

"Oh, here he is ...," said Ryan.

Geethanjali looked up to see a young man jogging towards them with a backpack.

"Do you think he will be able to handle it?"

"Let us see, that's why we're here. It's just a casual meeting, but this guy Sathish is kind of brilliant. And we have our financial constraints."

Wow Ryan has so much confidence in this Sathish and his friends. Where did he come across him?

"Hello Ryan Anna," he said as he neared them.

"Hello Akka," he flashed a huge smile at her too.

Hmmm... This is too casual. His face is familiar thought Geethanjali, but she could hardly place him.

"Let's sit," Ryan and Sathish joined Geethanjali on the broken log.

"Buy some peanuts Anna..." A vendor came towards them.

"Later...," said the young boy.

"So, the others have not been able to make it?" inquired Ryan.

"Sorry Anna ...as I was saying last night...Jacob had to be by the side of his father since an operation has been scheduled for him and Govind's only sister delivered a baby today...so he had to leave today... he has no father, so he is like their family head. But we did not want to postpone this initial meeting."

"Oh ok Sathish ... let's begin,"

Sathish pulled open his laptop from his backpack and logged in.

"Akka, please take a look at these released applications... this was built by us and please see the reviews on them.

He walked them through the applications and the tech stack behind them.

"Sathish, thanks for walking through these ... in our case, the user interface for us needs to be very simple and user-friendly. Our end users would primarily be the elderly folks ...our project is a dream for us ... we need to make it happen to make the dreams of our founder come true...."

And then the words stopped from Geetha's mouth.

Staring before her was the screen which exactly replicated one of the end-user prototype forms.

"Try it Geetha," smiled Ryan.

She slowly tapped the options on the menu, her fingers shivering a bit... Her paper prototype on My medicine Tracker was an actual working piece of software.

"Anna had shared one of your process flows and we built this first version for you to see"

"Thanks Sathish!"

"Good Job Sathish,"

Ryan towards Geetha.

"Let me schedule a call with our management once your friends are back." Geetha answered.

"Thank you Akka...and Anna! Thanks for giving me and my friends the opportunity...It's also our dream to make it a success."

"And now it's time for the roasted peanuts," he laughed as he hailed a vendor.

"Come on let's toast to our future success," joked Sathish as he handed out the peanut and chickpeas parcels to them.

The trio relaxed for a while, slowly becoming aware of the show that nature was putting out for them. The waves lashed back and forth towards the shore.

"So, how are the beaches in Florida, Anna?" Sathish broke the silence first

"Spent many summers sailing around. Let's see. I surely

have quite some pictures with me. In fact, my sister, just last week scanned and sent a few of the older pictures and shared our early days videos too," He pulled out his phone and began to scan through his Photos collections.

"So Akka, I have not seen you in the Orphanage since that first day we went together?" continued to chat Sathish turning towards Geetha.

Orphanage since that first day we went together? Geetha looked up in surprise and then the pieces all came together realizing then as to why he looked so familiar.

"Oh, are you that, SATHISH ???"

But, what a stark contrast to that bearded, listless man she had seen then versus a throbbing, confident young live wire that she was seeing now.

"Oh my gosh, you did not realize who he was all this time?" Ryan looked up in surprise

"Oh Anna, that should not be a surprise. I can totally understand. I was a total fool then... a fool drowned in the needless sea of love if I may say... a very dark period in my life... I just hate that love!" the young man muttered turning a little serious and agitated.

"Oh no, my buddy, love is not bad. There is no need to hate it and go off on another extreme. In fact, it's not the cause for the problems," gently interjected Ryan.

"But Anna, I thought even you were of that opinion too. I thought I heard you say that sometime back ...,"

"Well yes...true maybe initially...but then I thought...and realized that's not the problem,"

Geetha just sat quietly watching the two men exchange their views. This was not her area of expertise.

"Here, take a look at this," Ryan held out his phone to both Sathish and Geetha.

"Wow splendid waters!" Sathish exclaimed switching out of his seriousness.

"Is this Florida? And such a cool boat! "

A family, of apparently two children and parents, stood posing in against the back drop of a boat, a picture of perfect happiness and excitement.

"Who are they, Anna?"

"Who are they Ryan?"

"Wait, let me show the video actually,"

The two kids were seated and waving with happiness. The father at the helm of the steering, gave another wave followed by the mother.

"These folks are actually my folks -my parents and that is me and my little sister. It was our first maiden trip on our very own boat and yes it was my father's first day out in the sea after his boat training,"

"Oh little Ryan," Geetha looked with interest.

"Wow, cool!" Sathish devoured with excitement.

But the focus on the video shifted to an object outside the porthole. Apparently little Ryan was the camera man filming the adventure.

"Well look at that," Ryan said zooming on that object.

"A ship...big one...looks like a freight ship....," she volunteered wondering why Ryan was showing that explicitly to them.

And then their hearts skipped a beat. The blue waters had vanished...suddenly out of nowhere greyish monstrous waves appeared to be rolling outside and rushing in apparently in the boat's direction. Everything just happened in a few seconds. The little boat seemed to change direction and the bow appeared to go perpendicular trying to break off the waves at it's maximum speed. The boat appeared to rise with the crest of the waves and also fall flat down with a tremendous force. Loose objects were seen flying around. A loud thud was heard and the picture went blank. Terrified cries of a little girl were heard.

Whatever was that? What had just happened? Geetha and Sathish turned towards Ryan in shocked silence.

"Well my friends, those were breaking waves that were sent by the wake of the cargo ship which had passed in the distance probably 15 mins before then and

my dad's attempt at taking on the wave head on."

"Oh Anna, all that wake was caused by that cargo ship which you just showed us ? that must have been an unnerving first experience for all of you!"

"Yes indeed, Sathish,"

"Ryan ... is boating so risky?"

"Oh! everything has risks Geetha,"

"So, what happened after it? Trust, you'll reached safely? Did you give up boating?"

"Oh nopes, boating is perfectly nice. In fact, doing any activity on the water gives you a different perspective of life ...,"

"But...,"

"We love our boat. We just were not doing things right. Being amateurs at boating, we had no business of going out in the bay. We had paid no heed to the rules of the sea. I remember my dad later realized that it also had been a new moon day when tides are still stronger, so many factors were conveniently ignored.”

“Oh...”

“Anyways, we then removed our boat out of that salt water marina and moved it into a marina on the lake. The lake is obviously calmer and my father and mother both joined a number of additional boating classes and built their experience,”

“Oh, ok...,”

“And that my friend is how we handle any situation in life too ...holds good for love too,”

Sathish looked perplexed.

“So, one must become experienced in love before loving?” he joked.

“Oh no Sathish. I think that Ryan, by experience here, is alluding to the maturity of the mind, how it is trained to process, react and respond to any situations -happy or sad- the tides and currents in our life -calm or choppy situations that we may need to encounter...,”

“Spot on Geetha!” Ryan’s eyes twinkled.

“The waters are magnificent. Boating in those waters is uplifting. Life is even beyond magnificent. And love which you might encounter in that life is special.”

“Gosh...maybe we need to design an application for true love now ...Maybe you can give the specs for it Akka?,” Sathish smiled.

“Oh no Sathish, we do not need any complex algorithm for love or for any other pressing matter in our lives...,”

And then she broke into a mischievous smile as Ryan’s eyes sparkled with the same mischievous thought. They both turned towards Sathish and broke out the golden prescription to him,

"Use your prefrontal cortex. Do not use your amygdala!"

The beach reverberated with their laughter and the few other people in the beach looked out curiously and amusedly at them.

25

THE RECEPTION

THE FESTIVE beats of the mirdingham[17] alternating with the mesmerizing nadhaswaram rendition along with the melodious notes from the flute filled the marriage hall providing a musical treat to the attendees of Geethanjali's younger sister's reception.

Geethanjali slowly entered the hall scanning the crowd of attendees to look for any familiar faces. Yes, she was a little, in fact quite a bit deliberately detained with various odd jobs at home, so as to not accompany the main wedding party, while they set forth to the hall first. But she was not complaining. Well, if people hold forth to their superstitions, so be it. She was determined to enjoy the festivities. Her face broke into a thankful smile as she spotted her aunt.

---

17   mirdingham-a type of percussion instrument

"Hello aunty! When did you come? But why are you sitting over here in the back? Come along. There are so many places still in the front."

"Hello Geethanjali... that's okay, the music is clear over here."

"Oh... I did not know that you are such a fan of our classical music." And then it dawned on her.

"Oh yes... We are in the same boat." she laughed.

Widows and divorcees are generally not welcome invitees to auspicious events.

"Let's listen to the music. Oh, we have the mathalam too." She said sitting down on the chair besides her aunt.

"My goodness Geethanjali!" gasped her aunt.

"What happened Aunty?"

"It's been ages, many years since I've seen you dressed up like this."

"Oh, this ..." smiled Geethanjali looking down at her lovely navy blue Kanjeevaram silk saree and her matching sapphire necklace and bangles and her ear rings.

"Well...all these sarees and jewels were gathering dust. So, it's high time at least they have a ball," grinned Geethanjali.

"Well, this is the niece I knew before ...happy, spirited but a little thoughtful girl ...I am very happy today Geetha."

"Oh aunty...!"

"So Geetha, did you invite any of your colleagues.?"

"Oh yes Aunty. Appa gave me a few invitations. But nobody would be coming. All of the staff in the admin and finance department have other weddings to attend too. It's supposedly a super auspicious day today. Sathish and co also have a business meeting in Bangalore."

"Well.. how about Dr. Ryan.?"

"Oh Ryan...well yes, he too will not be coming. There is a reception of another doctor colleague's sister which he had earlier accepted already."

"Oh, he will come then."

"Oh no Aunty, the other reception is held in a totally opposite direction. So, he cannot make it to both the places on the same evening. Also, even yesterday evening I saw Dr Priya reminding him of her sister's reception today."

"Oh Geetha ...I just noticed...you have kept kunkum on the forehead ...you look so sweet."

"Oh yes Aunty, Ryan was asking the other day why I never wear it. So, I just thought and kept it today."

"Oh, is that so," smiled the Aunt, trying hard to remain nonchalant, her eyes now fixed on the entrance door.

"Whom are you looking out for Aunty?" wondered Geethanjali following the direction of her Aunt's eyes and for a moment her heart danced to the beat of the mridangam.

There he stood, a most different looking Ryan. not in his hospital scrubs but dressed in a navy blue suit and sporting a silk tie and looking most handsome.

"Wow he came...!"

"Geetha ...go welcome him first. I cannot get up and walk fast enough," her Aunt nudged her.

As Ryan stood admiring the karkandu[18] display on the silver tray and slowly picked the karkandu from the welcome tray, his bent hair was sprayed down by a sudden jet of water.

"Wow," he looked up his consternation evaporating to

---

18   karkandu-rock sugar candy

amusement as he saw Geetha holding the paneer sombhu[19], in her hands.

"Welcome!" she smiled.

"Well...indeed a nice welcome....,"

"Well I thought you would like rose water...I saw you one day talk about the benefits of rose water to a patient.."

"Oh really...,"

"Hey, did you give Anna lots of karkandu...he will tell you all about it's medicinal benefits...." She turned towards the children who were standing in the welcome station.

"Oh Geetha...please that's enough...Anyways...that's panarkarkandu.. But where did you suddenly come from ? I did not see you surely a minute ago anywhere over here."

"Well to say in little Dhammu's words maybe, I was propelled by a turbo boost from a jet engine...," and then her playful banter stopped as she saw his sparkling blue eyes gazing at her.

And then to her surprise he folded his hands and said "Vanakkam[20],"

"Vanakkam" she folded her hands too and they tried to laugh off the awkwardness and some undefinable sense of delirious happiness.

"Welcome Doctor,,,. Welcome" Mrs. Shyamala Sundaram greeted the doctor effusively folding her hands in the traditional vanakkam.

Geetha amusedly watched Ryan return the Vanakkam too,

"Hello Mrs. Sundaram. How are you doing?" And he added, "Also how are your buddies?"

---

19   paneer sombhu-rose water pot
20   Vanakkam-Hello with folded hands

"I am so happy. Oh doctor...what can I say...?"

Mrs. Shyamala Sundaram again folded her hands, but this time it was to say ...

"Thank you Doctor...Thanks ...Thanks so much...I will be eternally grateful"

"Oh no Mrs. Sundaram ...it's just my job...,"

"Well ...more days are good now...! I am so scared that this is a dream," she contemplated.

"Well, be rest assured, Mrs. Sundaram, good days are here to stay."

"Thank you doctor!"

"Oh, let's not stand, Geetha please seat him. And let me find the server to get some juice for Doctor Ryan."

"Oh no Mrs. Sundaram ...please do not bother...,"

"Oh doctor...it's one of my good days today, walking is a good exercise too as you advised the other day!"

"Oh wow...I am so happy that she feels so well," he turned towards Geetha as they watched her walk in the direction of the dining hall.

"Thank You Ryan for that,"

"Well, please do not get started with your share of praises... so where do I sit?"

"Oh, you want to sit?"

"Well, do you want me to stand?"

"Oh, I do not mean that. I just thought that you would be in a hurry to...,"

"Hurry to...?"

"I recall you mentioning that today was Dr Priya's sister's reception and she was very particular that you attend it," slowly blurted out Geetha.

"Oh that? I surely cannot be in two places at the same time in two different ends of the city...,"

"Oh, and surely you knew better," his blue twinkling eyes again met her's.

"Thanks," she managed to say.

"Come on Anni[21], this is Dr. Ryan." Her aunt's voice sounded from behind. She had found and brought Geetha's mother to meet Dr. Ryan.

Geetha turned back excitedly.

"Ryan .... this is my Amma," interjected Geetha too.

Her mother was surprised to hear her address a doctor at the hospital she worked for, so casually by his first name.

And she was even more surprised when that handsome doctor. folded his hands and said

"Vanakkam."

"Vanakkam," she smiled, "Welcome Dr. Ryan. We are so happy that you were able to come and grace this occasion. Anni (my sister in law) has been always been singing praises about the way you have helped her with her health issues."

"Oh...that's my profession,"

"Have you taken him to meet the couple?" she quizzed Mrs. Sundaram

"Not yet, amma ...he just arrived." answered Geetha instead.

"That's all right...Akka please take care of Dr. Ryan...the crowds are less now, so please take him to meet the couple now." she continued to address her sister in law.

"And Geetha, we need you in the dining hall."

"Akila..." sounded a voice behind and she excused herself,

---

21   Anni-sister-in-law

but not before turning towards Geetha with a momentary disapproving look to her perplexed daughter.

"Come Ryan... Come on aunty.. Let's go meet the bridal couple..."

"I've already met them Geetha... You and Ryan can go ...," answered her Aunt.

"That's all right aunty. Please come along too," insisted Geetha too suddenly feeling conscious of trooping down the wedding hall alone with Ryan. She had an uneasy feeling that he was already the center of attraction and there were quite some curious thoughts and eyes already turned in their direction. And possibly that was the cause for her mother's disapproving look too.

I need to probably be a bit more formal she thought. But before she could be bothered to go down this thought lane any further her thoughts were abruptly stopped in it's tracks.

A veena musical had just started...This was another favorite song of her's.

"Ryan," she whispered excitedly, "this is the instrumental of the song...

"Oh yes another song about your favorite hero... It's about the King Karna... extolling his virtues... Am I not right?"

"What... How did you know???"

"Well I saw the movie..,"

"What???"

"Well...guess I had to see it after you give such a glowing account of his valor and virtues."

"Unbelievable...." smiled Geetha.

"Actually, there were quite some portions I skipped. It would have helped if there were subtitles. But I remember seeing this song. And it was very powerful....,"

"Here we come..." interrupted her aunt. "And here is your Appa too."

Oh Appa, thought Geetha. Will he gave her the odd looks too like her mother she wondered.

"Anna, meet Dr. Ryan," introduced Mrs. Shyamala to Mr. Sundaram.

The two men shook hands. Ryan met the couple and handed over the gift.

"Sir, please stand... A photo please," the photographer called out.

Geetha turned an anxious eye towards her father. Well, he seems to look normal. Oh, he is turning in Ryan's direction again. I cannot really make out, she thought and unconsciously stood near Ryan for the picture.

"You're looking so sweet, but pretty darn serious." A soft voice interrupted her thoughts, "Let out your sweet smile too."

"Oh," she blushed.

And the flash from the camera struck all their smiling faces.

26

PANNIYARAMS...AND MORE

RYAN AND Mrs. Shyamala entered the dining hall. It was nearly an hour since Geethanjali had vanished to perform the suddenly assigned wedding chores. The dining hall was bustling with guests moving in and out of the dining hall. The catering staff scrambled nimbly with aromatic dishes. Ryan scanned around in all directions but could not see Geethanjali anywhere there too.

"Let's save a place for Geetha," he said as he and Geethanjali's aunt sat down for the reception dinner.

"Good idea," smiled the aunt.

"Please eat... Dr. Ryan....,"

Ryan looked at the banana leaf spread in front of him filled with colorful and aromatic food.

"Wow ...this is going to be a delicious feast." He took

one more look for Geethanjali and decided to begin eating.

He took his first bite preparing his senses to be floored. But no, his enthusiasm for the food diminished. How was he to eat all of this, his senses panicked. Was this food cooked with spices or spices cooked with food?

And then miraculously a member of the catering staff came forward with a small vessel and poured copious amounts of ghee on his food.

"Thank you," he looked up to also see a smiling Geethanjali standing beside the boy.

"Saw that your lacrimal glands were going to be very busy,"

Ryan smiled sheepishly.

"Ah ... You're finally back Geetha... What happened? You were gone for quite a while. Is everything okay?"

"Oh yes Aunty. There were some pending arrangements and changes to be made for tomorrow's morning ceremony."

"So, are you all done now? Come join us for dinner. Ryan saved a seat for you."

"Oh thank you..," smiled Geethanjali sliding into the chair and turning towards Ryan.

"It should be better now, try it now "

He mixed the ghee into the rice and gingerly took a brave bite. "Much better and actually nice," he smiled thankfully.

"Geetha... Ryan has been filling my ears with your guys novel Health Buddy program."

"And I've got your aunt to sign for it,"

"Oh really?"

"And I told her not to worry. There would be no extra hospital visits. It's purely from a monitoring point of view to ensure that we are on the right track for maintenance and alleviation of her issues."

And then he stopped. A slow, quiet groan escape from his mouth. He had bit into a hot red chili inadvertently.

"Have the sweet, doctor," advised her aunt.

Ryan looked warily at the orange spiraled sweet ...the great jalebi ... he was not a fan of it.

"Quick, eat this," another rushed voice advised him and his eyes widened in surprise, evaporating his tears.

"Panniyaram," he quizzed as he munched into them.

"Oh yes, we had a family prayer function in the morning at home for which we had prepared Paniyarams. And then I remembered your fondness for it. So, I saved up a few to give it to you."

"Thanks," said Ryan happily munching the sweet desert.

"Excuse me," said Geetha's aunt and got up to go wash her hands.

And then Ryan turned towards Geethanjali. His twinkling and teasing look is back. What was he going to say wondered Geethanjali.

"So, you knew I would come,"

"Oh my," blushed Geethanjali inwardly wondering how many more times was she going to blush that evening.

The two of them also finished their dinner and walked to find Mrs. Sundaram. They saw her surrounded by a group of ladies and did not want to disturb her.

"So, what shall we do now?" They stood wondering, when they saw two little children waving out to them.

"Come Anna, come Akka...," beckoned the kids.

"Can you please help us open this box?" They asked, handing Geethanjali a steel box.

"Oh, whatever is in it? It looks so old too," wondered Geethanjali.

"It's so tight," she struggled with it.

"Let me try," volunteered Ryan and then after a couple of pulls he was able to open the lid of the steel box.

There was an assortment of shells in it.

"Are you going to play, palangulli?[22]" quizzed Geetha.

"Yes...," The children's eyes gleamed.

"Have fun..," Ryan handed over the box to the children.

"Thank You," said the children and sat down in their little world of excitement and fun play. Another group of active kids rather chose to play with a ball. They watched the kids play boisterously with amusement.

"So Geetha, who do you think enjoys the most in these wedding functions?"

"Well, ideally it should be the bride and bridegroom," she thought slowly,

"But guess not," she saw Ryan's eyes twinkling. A ball suddenly came whizzing past them.

"I think it's these young ones. it's an arena to get together with all the cousins and relatives and build memories."

"Yes, for other guests too..."

"I suppose so," she smiled as her phone suddenly rang.
paadavaa paadavaa ....

"Excuse me," she said as she reached out for the phone in
her handbag.

"Oh, just a marketing call," she murmured as she saw the number flash on the display and put it away

---

22 palangulli-two player wooden board game

"Hey, you changed your ring tone... And this sounds very happy,"

"Oh yes," she smiled.

"So, what's special about this song?" He quizzed as he picked up the ball which had rolled his feet.

"Oh, nothing really significant... It's just a melodious happy song."

"Uncle, it's from Little john." volunteered a small kid as she came to fetch the ball from Ryan.

"Thanks for the info," smiled Ryan surprised to see that the little ones were tuned in to their surroundings even while playing.

"But wait... Little John?" puzzled Ryan addressing to Geetha. "Which historical figure is this?"

"Historical figure....?" The kids burst out laughing.

Geetha sat stunned wondering at what else the kids would utter.

"Go and play..." she tried shooing them away. But they stood chatting. Possibly their little legs were tired with all the play and were now just interested in chatting.

"Google it uncle..,"

"It's just a young tourist who loves an Indian girl on his visit," cried out a few other kids bursting out in laughter.

"My goodness," felt an embarrassed Geetha. She turned towards Ryan.

"So, no king ...this time...," he burst out laughing.

"No historical figure," she burst out laughing too in return and together they decided to just see the comedy behind it and not read any further into it, blissfully unaware of the eyes in the wedding crowd that had turned in their direction.

27

PRESENTING THE HEALTH BUDDY

MR. AROKIYASWAMY paused for a couple of minutes scanning the reactions on the faces of the assembled reporters. Then pointing to the garlanded picture of the founder in the room he continued, "Our founder Dr. Kamaraj was a doctor who treated his patients as his brother, as his sister, as his father or grandfather or grandmother or in other words as his own kith and kin. When one has that attitude then the care and level of involvement in his patient's well-being is multiplied. He ensured that all the folks in his village had the best preventive medical measures in place. He was a firm advocate of the principle that prevention is better than cure and if one was not so lucky then he took pains to find out a quick cure for it."

"And now, fast forward to nearly a century later to this

supercharged world, that we now live in. Given our population growth demands and the nature of our health concerns it is nearly impossible or impractical for the doctor to treat everybody with that kind of relationship or connection."

"But we wanted to harness the power of technology that we have to reach out to our patients and for our patients to reach back to us so that together we partner entirely in taking the optimal structured treatment plan for our patients."

Oh, my turn now, thought Geethanjali as Mr. Arokiyaswamy stood up and signaled the helpers to pass the models of the health buddy to the assembled reporters. She turned to Dr. Ryan automatically. She was feeling happy and confident, but still turned towards him for his encouraging smile too.

He gave her his encouraging smile and thumbs-up and slowly whispered, "You are the best!"

"I will now have Ms. Geethanjali the real architect and brain behind this concept and product to give a walk-through of this product."

Geethanjali took the control of the presentation.

"Thank you, Mr. Arokiyaswamy." And she turned towards the reporters.

"Welcome folks to this personal world of My health Buddy!"

She paused for a couple of minutes to ensure that everyone had their own personal model of the health buddy. Her eyes again unconsciously turned in Ryan's direction.

A double thumbs up sign again greeted her.

"Well, are you all excited to get the first peek into our Health Buddy."

"Oh yes!" cheered the reporters.

"Well then here we go...without much further ado, requesting all of you to please press the little green button on your device,"

The users were landed into the home screen. A very simple and pleasing dashboard popped up.

On the home screen you will see a dashboard pop up. I will get to this in a couple of minutes. Also, on the home screen you will also see many other options on the left side called the menu options.

The audience nodded.

The first menu option called the My Symptoms Tracker is the screen where in the patient's symptoms and health concerns are logged with the rating scale initially in the first visit of the patient by the staff, and then needs to be entered in by the patient during the treatment period.

"Daily?" questioned a reporter

"Yes, that's right or if needed even earlier, as determined by the treatment plan laid out by the doctor."

"The next menu tab is My prescriptions wherein the patient's prescribed medication is initially logged in and entered by the hospital staff and then subsequently the patient logs in their intake of the medicines. Here we have features built in such as automated personalized reminders for any missed medications. And if a person ignores the reminders then they get a call from our nurses after a grace period of few hours depending on the criticality of the medicine, to check with the patient as to what's going on.

Remember... MrArokiyaswamy said a fundamental promise and our hospital goal or vision is to ensure an optimal structured treatment collaborated plan for our patients. And this is one such building block to ensure this goal. It helps to ensure that our treatment plan is on track or if anything needs to be tweaked.

And, this is also a building block in ensuring a continuous relationship with the patient."

"Apart from medications we may have recommended other integrative therapies or lifestyle changes. This is tracked in the Other Treatment tab. And the correlation between the Symptoms and Treatment plan is what appears as a dashboard summary in the home page. In other words, it displays the success of our treatment plan versus the symptoms.

We have two other tabs- the diagnostic Tab which holds the copies of all the diagnostic reports taken for the patient. And lastly the recordings tab holds any specific instructions to the patient such as when to take the medicines etc by the doctors or maybe the recording of an exercise demo by the physiotherapist for the patient's playback reference.

"So, this my friends, is our health buddy."

"Any questions?" asked Geetha scanning the reporters faces. .

One lady raised her hand.

"Thank you for the details. I do see the benefits. Why did we need to have a separate device for this? Will this not increase the cost unnecessarily for the patients?"

"Well our primary focus was on extending this level of collaborated care to our elderly patients. And given the demographics of these patients that we were focusing on. not all of them had access to a smart phone with robust capabilities or ever had a reliable Wi-Fi connection when their children where away at work. Also, we wanted to stress the importance of this as a special personal health specific device. We wanted our application to be as user-friendly as possible. The display size should be reasonably comfortable to the eye, ergonomic to handle and above all minus any technical shortcomings of the hardware. The answer was our own device running our application. Besides, it will be an one-time re-useable investment"

"Yes, it is indeed light and user-friendly. Agreed, the lady reporter.

Another reporter raised his hand.

"Does this not increase the time spent in the first visit for the patient with all this set up processes etc.?"

"Of course, you're right. But this is time well spent. The savings in terms of time would be definitely seen and appreciated in the subsequent visits. The patient's progress is known beforehand to the doctor during the treatment period. In some cases, this would help a doctor determine the next treatment and skip or delay the follow-up doctor appointment itself."

The reporters nodded.

"And above all, can you guess, what is the best benefit from this device in terms of time?"

A number of hands raised up in the audience.

"Shorter recovery period !"

"Perfect! Yes there will be a considerable reduction in the recovery period,"

"We also have amongst us a couple of patients who participated in the testing.They have kindly consented to answer any usage related feedback questions that you'll might request for"

"Thank you for being here today with us... Mrs. Ramani and her daughter Ms Yashoda."

"The pleasure is ours," said the young daughter.

"All that I have to say is... this is AMAZING .It has made us totally conscious and educated of my mother's health and we feel that we are in safe hands for the best possible treatment... In fact, I'm thinking of signing up too from a preventive care perspective," she said and sat down.

"Oh, me too," smiled back the reporters switching off their recording devices.

"We will be bringing our parents too."

Many reporters chimed in appreciatively,

"We truly think it is a one stop solution for tracking our medical health concerns to recovery."

"Thank you for your support," smiled Geetha turning over to Mr. Arokiyaswamy to give his closing remarks.

She slipped down into a chair with a thankful sigh turning towards Ryan.

"I think we are in the cusp of a breakthrough in the digitalization of personalized complete and accountable patient care," he whispered.

Before she could reply, his pager buzzed. "Got to go." he said and got up, signaling that he would message her.

She nodded.

A few minutes later, her phone gave a mild hop as if it was also hopping in excitement.

"Let's celebrate. Let's go out for dinner," the message read.

Dinner? she wondered.

"Yes!" she typed smilingly.

28

HAPPY MOMENTS

G EETHA WAS reviewing the expense files to be submitted to the auditor when the phone rang.

"Could it be Ryan so soon?" she smiled eagerly reaching out for her phone.

"Hello," her sister's voice sounded in a rush, "Geetha... please come home immediately."

"Oh, what happened? Is everything all right?"

"Oh no time to explain on the phone... Just start at once..." pleaded the voice at the other end.

"All right," said a surprised and startled Geetha and hurried out after dashing a quick excuse note to her manager.

As she made her way to the elevator, she hurriedly messaged Ryan.

"Go to go home now. May not be back in time for lunch

... will meet up once I am back..."

And as she walked down the hospital lobby, she saw Ryan in conversation with Dr Priya.

Dr. Priya was apparently in high spirits and her chuckles of laughter reached all the way to a rushing Geetha.

Should she call out to him she thought. Oh no, let's not disturb now she dismissed the thought and she passed by quietly. And then a mischievous thought entered her head and she turned back to see Ryan.

She was pleased with what she saw. Yes, he was smiling back in response to Dr. Priya's chatter. But it was purely a polite smile. That special smile with his blue twinkling eyes and radiant face were surely only for her she thought happily and possessively.

He is my best friend. He is my...

As she stepped out of the hospital entrance the security guard greeted her. "Shall I call for an auto Madam?" He asked.

"Yes please," she answered her train of thoughts broken.

29

WHAT?

"Aah ...thankfully you came in time," greeted a beaming Renuka.

"Renu..." began Geethanjali, but before either of the sisters could talk further....

"Tag," a piercing shriek sounded as two kids zoomed past the sisters.

"Tag! You are it,"cried out little Arjun catching little Suja.

"No," squealed Suja and escaped into another room.

"Oh, your sister-in-law's kids are here? What's up? Is she here?" Geetha lowered her voice to a whisper looking around but not catching anyone else nearby in sight.

"Kids, go inside and play quietly in Geetha Aunty's room," Renuka shooed the little kids away.

And then the aromatic smell of ghee wafted through the

air.

"Wow... ever since you are married, you are being treated as the guest of honor. Amma is always preparing feasts for you guys."

"So, what is the treat Amma for Renuka today?" teased Geetha walking into the kitchen.

"It's not for me Akka, it's for you...!"

"Me?" said a surprised Geetha catching a glimpse of the goodies being tossed and fried in the ghee.

Wow, is it telepathy wondered Geethanjali. Did her folks indeed sense her happiness at today's work presentation.? Ryan would love it she continued to think.

"Thank you Amma," she said and took the ladle from her and started placing them inside a tiffin box.

"What are you doing, Geetha?" questioned her mother.

"Oh, for the hospital staff Amma,"

"What...oh no...this is not for your work place ... I'm doing it for the bridegroom party coming soon."

"Bridegroom party?" asked Geetha her smile vanishing and dreading what she might hear.

"Your little sister is now so grown up. She's playing match-maker for you. She has apparently spoken to her mother-in-law about you and thus her mother-in-law now has arranged for this alliance." gushed her mother, oblivious of the scope of emotions behind Geetha's stunned face.

"They will be here any time soon. So first please go and get ready," And then her mother slowly paused as she worried how her daughter would react to the bridegroom's situation.

"The bridegroom is a very wealthy businessman. He is a widower with two daughters in their teens."

She looked up to see Geetha's face. It still had the same blank countenance.

"The age difference is a little high around 12 years," she continued. "but Renuka's mother-in-law says he will look younger. Also, she vouches for his wealth and family heritage."

Again, she looked up to see Geetha's face. It still had the same blank countenance.

"So, Geetha...?"

"I never asked you for details...." She answered slowly finding her words.

"Oh yes... We know you Geetha. You will agree to anyone we say. But I wanted you to have all the details." sighed her mom turning to her frying pan and to ladle out the paniyarams.

"And Akka, I know that you would be a good mother. I told that to my mother-in-law." added Renuka with her inputs.

"Alright Geetha...go and get ready,"

"Amma, I never asked you for details because I do not need the details. I never asked anybody to find me a husband."

The mom dropped down her ladle in surprise.

"I'm not going to parade myself in front of this crazy bride-groom party of your's!" She lashed out at Renuka.

"I have work to do. I am leaving,"

At that moment a car horn sounded in their portico.

"Akka, my mother-in-law must have come. Let's discuss this afterwards. Please just see them. Please do not let me down in front of my mother-in-law. She has arranged this alliance and will not take it lightly if you refuse to see them!"

"Besides, it's just a bride seeing function. We will not commit anything," pleaded her mother.

30

HUMAN VOLCANO

GEETHANJALI SEETHING inwardly like a dormant volcano sat down along with her sister observing painfully the exchange of information between her family and the bridegroom party. Her eyes moved to the mother of the suitor. She was looking quiet and reserved. Although she was quiet, she had brought along her elder sister who compensated with her incessant talk and gathering of information on Geethanjali and her family.

My nephew is a wonderful father. His late wife was a loving mother a perfect daughter-in-law. She extorted the virtues of her sister's son

"He is so busy. He couldn't come. But he's fine with our decision and the children's decision. The children need to like the future mother."

Geetha painfully swallowed the emotion that came up her throat. Thank goodness Mr. eligible man never graced the occasion too, she thought.

And then she slowly took a look at the daughters. The two teenagers were busy browsing or probably playing something on the phone. Good, they are in their own world she thought. But no, the very next minute they looked up directly at her and exchanged words between themselves and shot laughing looks at each while their hands continued to work on the phone.

Where the young ones too discussing her, she wondered. Geetha's eye darted for probably the umpteenth time on the wall clock.

Oh gosh it's 5 o'clock. Three hours had passed by and they have still not left. How can I now go back to the hospital, she calculated with weary frustration.

"We saw Ashok, very happy with this wife. They have a little son too..." She heard the visitor's talks jolting her out of the calculations. Ashok ??? Which Ashok? Oh gosh , that man who had been the dark, finished chapter in her life.

Wow, what is this lady trying to insinuate now? crossed Geetha's mind.

Is she trying to say that Ashok was a great husband material and that she was at fault? Or was she trying to glean information on why she did not have a child? Oh gosh, when will they leave? her heart cried.

It was just this morning that I was so happy, she thought. It was the confident me who was sitting in the conference room along with my managing director answering questions and giving a business presentation to reporters from reputed newspapers. And now by the evening, I am reduced to a person sitting in her own home and squirming at the questions and looks from these absolute strangers come in the guise of prospective alliance. Which is for real? She panicked. But thinking of her workplace assuaged the fire within her. Would Ryan have finished his appointments? What will he be doing? And then she heard her phone ring from her room.

"Oh... Let me get it," she said glad to get an excuse to get out of the living room.

But her father stopped her sternly.

"Never mind, Geetha,"

And the phone probably too did not dare to disobey her father that it stopped ringing then. But no, the phone did have its own mind. She gleefully heard it ring again.

"Let Renuka answer it," her father's voice boomed.

"Yes Appa," said Renuka breezing into her sister's bedroom to answer the phone.

Who could it be? thought Geetha. Ryan...? She hoped, it was.

31

SHOCKS FOR RYAN

RYAN HAD finished all his appointments quite early and was wrapping his last review of the patient progress on the Health Buddy program, when the clock struck 5 PM. "Nice," he introspected.

Will it not be wonderful if there were no illness in this world and the hospitals were places to come for just well care and preventive care appointments.

And then the phone rang. Okay it must be Geetha finally, he smiled and reached out for the phone. But he was pleasantly surprised to see it was a call from back home.

"Mom!" He greeted cheerfully but was surprised at the odd time she was calling. It would be just early morning there. And then his face froze as he tried to absorb what his mom had conveyed.

"Mom be brave. It's good that you got him hospitalized in time. Everything will be all right. I will be right there tomorrow." saying he hung up the phone.

He called up his friends who were working at the same hospital and inquired on his father's real condition.

Now for the travel agent... His hands were shaking as he searched his contacts list for the travel agent.

"Flight ticket to Florida for tonight please," he spoke trying to sound calm.

"That would be $4000 for economy, Sir," said the voice on the other end.

"That's fine," he said continuing to share the other details for the booking.

All right flight and taxi has been booked. What else? His mind thought in a frenzy.

Need to get my passport from home. And then he broke down. He had told his mother to be brave and that everything would be all right. But would it be? His father had had a massive heart attack when he had gone out for his morning jog. And he was still in the emergency room.

"Oh God," he cried unable to control himself. He was a doctor. But now as he was crying out for his father, he was reduced to just a little son. His memories of his father zoomed past him. He heard a knock on the door. It was the hospital attendant.

"Doctor Sir, is everything all right?"

"Oh yes," answered back Dr. Ryan.

I must control myself, he thought. Oh, what am I to do? Aah...let me talk to Geetha. In that state of haze, he wanted to share his sorrow with Geetha. She will know the right things to say and reached out for his phone and called her number.

But nobody answered his phone. He tried again and this time it was answered.

"Geetha..." he began.

"Hello, I'm her sister," announced the voice on the other end.

"I'm calling from the hospital," he began.

"Oh, we have a family function at home and she may not be able to come in today. Should I take a message?"

"Yes please. I am Dr. Ryan. Can you please tell her to call me as soon as possible. It's urgent..." he rushed through when he stopped with a halt.

"Oh Dr. Ryan. I know you. How are you? You are a good friend for Geethanjali. Actually, the prospective bridegroom's family for her is visiting us now and we will be having the Poochoodhal function shortly too."

"Poochoodhal?"

"Oh... It's kind of an engagement- an agreement between both the families to tie the knot," the sister clarified.

"Oh okay... then she will be busy..." He said feeling nauseous and his hands began trembling as he put down the phone.

What did he just hear now? The sister's voice kept echoing in his thoughts.

"You are a good friend,"

He tried to assimilate his feelings. Was I just a good friend?

Okay... her best friend he tried to reason himself. But engagement...? he thought, anger and disappointment slightly now raising their heads.

Well if she was my best friend, I should be happy for her and not be angry or disappointed that she did not tell me about it, he thought.

But he had grown so accustomed to being with her. She had become an integral part of his day to day life.

"Oh god!" He cried again. What was he going through? Whatever was happening? His world was turned topsy-turvy in the last one hour.

The phone again rang. It was the taxi driver reporting his arrival. Ryan washed his face and tried to steady himself. He called up Mr. Arokiyaswamy and left a voicemail on his family situation and dashed a hurried email to him. And then with trembling hands, his fingers messaged,

"Geetha.... Please call me when you see this. It's urgent. My dad has had a massive heart attack. I'm flying tonight to Florida. My flight is around midnight. Please call me anytime tonight unto them,"

He also messaged his contact details in US and email ID as he realized that they had not shared those details before. The phone rang again. He was hopeful that it was Geetha who had seen his message. No, it was not. It was Mr. Arokiyaswamy calling back.

"Whatever is she doing now? When will she call?" he sighed as he spoke to Mr. Arokiyaswamy.

32

FINAL STRAW

GEETHANJALI LOOKED expectantly at her sister as Renuka re-entered the living room.

"It was from the hospital and I informed that you would not be coming in," she said taking her place.

"So which hospital is this? I forgot the name." asked the boy's Aunt listening to this exchange.

"Arokya hospital," said her father.

"Oh, that's small one-near the Nungambakkam fly over," she said turning over to her sister.

"Small one..." Geetha's ears were burning. And then her eyes opened wide in disbelief. Those two girls had stepped into the dining room and were rummaging the contents of the refrigerator. They emerged with two bars of chocolate and started unwrapping the papers.

Wow... She thought... Nice set of manners.

And then she heard her cheerful father's voice say, "Geetha ... show your book collection to the children.."

My goodness, she winced in disbelief. Was he trying to bond her with the children? No way. She stayed firmly put in her place.

"Oh, I will show them Appa!" Renuka instead volunteered.

Or maybe I should have gone regretted Geetha at wasting the opportunity to get away. And then she finally heard the words she was longing to hear.

The bridegroom party announced that they were finally leaving.

"All right it's getting late and my nephew is still in the meeting. So, we will leave now."

The two girls emerged but now, not without making Geetha's blood boil even higher.

They were holding two of her favorite books from back school which she had secured as a general proficiency prize.

"I will take those," she said politely as she reached out to retrieve those books.

"Oh, we are going to take them home to read,"

"Surely they can have it?" supported the old Aunt coldly.

"Of course, sure." nodded her father

"But Appa... Those are my favorite..." began Geetha when she was cut short abruptly by her father

"That's all right." he said and walked the guests to the car.

"It's just a book," her mom whispered as she followed her husband to send away the guests.

"Yes.... You allowed them to take away just a book now," her inner voice sounded. Do not allow them to take away your life.

She retreated silently to her bedroom. The two little children were still busy playing in that room.

She found her phone precariously perched in the edge of the table. Couldn't her sister keep it back in the bag? she thought. Anyways, let me message Ryan.

And then her eyes stared back in disbelief. The message on the display simply read.

Please reinstall your operating system.

"Whatever happened to my phone?" she cried in dismay.

"Aunty..." The two children looked up sheepishly.

"We were just wanting to play some video games on your phone. So, we tried to enter some passwords for it."

"Come on Suja and Arjun. Let's leave," she heard Renuka, calling out to the children.

"Gosh... They probably had exceeded the incorrect password attempts and the device security feature had kicked in and had wiped the device clean."

"Oh God! This is the final straw", she sat down weakly burrowing her face in her hands.

33

CLOUDY MORNING

"Geetha ... I have prepared your favorite APPAMS for lunch today," Geetha's mom announced with pretended cheerfulness as her daughter entered into the kitchen the next morning.

But no smile escaped the daughter's lips. She just pulled a bowl and tumbler for her breakfast cereal. She still appeared grim and was probably still not ready to forget and forgive the previous evening.

"Geetha... Take your umbrella today. The monsoons are going to start and a low trough is already developing in the Bay of Bengal," her father announced peeking out of his newspaper.

"Okay," the daughter managed to murmur and mechanically poured the cereal into a bowl.

The mother and father exchanged glances at each other.

"The milk is cold," her mother interrupted, "let me warm it."

"It's okay," the daughter said and continued with the breakfast.

And then her mother dealt her trump card. She placed another tiffin box beside her lunchbox.

"It's paniyarams for your colleagues, just like you asked for yesterday,"

The spoon dropped from her daughter's mouth. And yes, the smile finally escaped from her daughter's lips.

"Amma...you needn't have done it. I just mentioned that since I saw you making it yesterday."

"Anyways...Thanks!" she said appreciating her mother's gesture. She couldn't continue her silent protest with her parents any longer. Hopefully it's an experience which will not repeat itself, she tried to console herself.

She eagerly opened the Tiffin box.

"Yes, perfectly browned and crispy," she commented.

"Just the way you like it," smiled back the mom.

"Oh, just the way Ryan will like it," smiled back Geethanjali oblivious of the now receding smile on her parents faces as they tried to process her answer.

A heavy cloud partially appeared to clear from her thoughts as her mind calculated that in a short while she will be back in the hospital and will be surprising Ryan with his newfound favorite treats.

The image of Ryan enjoying the Paniyarams, played upon her. Thinking of her workplace and thinking of Ryan lifted her spirits. Everything will be just alright after all she thought

Thus, twenty minutes later, a much more cheerful Geetha stepped out of her home. But as she looked up at the overcast sky, a feeling of unexplained uneasiness again clouded her spirits.

34

GET WELL MR RICHARSON...

THE PRAYER meeting at the Orphanage Home concluded. The children left the prayer hall and Geetha stood alone with the warden.

"Thanks Madam, for organizing this meeting to pray for the speeding recovery of Dr. Ryan's father Mr. Richardson,"

"It's the least we can do...but we need to be confident, that everything would be soon well for Dr. Ryan and his family."

Geetha smiled gratefully and picked up her bag wearily. Guess, this is the other facet of life, everything has become topsy turvy in the last 24 hours she sighed.

"Akka, wait....we have just finished the card...," little Kavitha rushed into the room.

Geetha took up the card from the little child.

Against the backdrop of a brilliant sunrise, were painted

many faces.

It's all of us from the Orphanage Akka, 20 children and then our warden and our 2 teachers and other staff members.

"Oh I see...now I can put the names on the faces ...guess this must be you ...this must be Mariam..,"

"Ah you are right Akka, and guess who is that person standing next to me...,"

"Oh...the teacher...,"

"No Akka ...that's you,"

"Oh...,"

Geetha flipped open the card curiously.

The words HAPPY 365 ! were neatly written on it.

"Akka, it's our Get Well Card from all of us to Ryan Anna's father,"

"Happy 365?"

"Yes Akka, we read that's the new upper limit for a healthy long human life,"

"Oh, I thought that it was 120 years,"

"Yes Akka, we also thought that too...but one of our teachers said she came across this new number in an article recently. And we thought, the higher it is, even better !"

"Wow..Dr Ryan's father would be so happy to see your little wishes expressed so thoughtfully,"

"We have all signed Akka. You alone need to sign it and then send it over to Dr. Ryan,"

"Oh,"

A bell sounded in the orphanage.

"Our dinner bell, Akka...Bye Akka..,"

"Bye,Good Night"

Geetha folded the card and carefully tucked it into a diary

in her bag. She did not want it to be creased. And it was then, that she realised with dismay.

"Where am I to send it to?"

I do not have his contact details in USA. The hospital records too did not seem to have any proper details. The very moment she had heard about his dad, she had rushed to the records section to get his contact information... but it was a strange disconnected tone that had filled her ears. Hopefully, he would contact her or someone in the hospital soon.

35

THE STORM AT HOME

"Thank you so much," said Geetha's mother Mrs Vasudevan to her neighbor Mrs.Lakshmi Narayan as she handed her all the postal mail and packages which she had been holding for Geetha's family while they had gone out of station.

"Please sit down. Let me bring you some hot coffee,"

"Oh, it's okay. You all must be tired after your journey,"

But hardly did the neighbor finish saying, than did Geetha's sister Renuka breeze into the room carrying a steaming hot cup of coffee.

"Have it, Aunty!"

Geetha watched her sister with amusement. Before her marriage she hardly used to step a foot into the kitchen and now she was waltzing her way in and out of the kitchen like a lifelong expert hostess.

"Thank you dear," said Mrs. Lakshmi Narayan. And as she took a sip of the hot coffee, she appeared to garner more energy to recount the impact of the monsoons on their city Chennai in the past fortnight.

"You were all so lucky to get away from this hardship we had over here," she began, "It was like we were all marooned in an island with no connection to the outer world. People were being rescued in boats. The Army had to come in with their helicopters. But humanity was at it's best. Strangers were helping complete strangers."

"Oh yes... We were trying to reach my sister-in-law Shyamala Anni and we were panicking as we could not reach her."

"Which locality was she in?"

"Virugambakkam."

"Oh yes... parts of that area were also affected by flooding."

"Yes, she had got her phone connection restored only today morning and we managed to contact her today only."

"Oh yes... In all parts of the city phone connections were down. Power was down. It was like living in the stone age." She sighed, "Anyways, how was your trip to your native town?"

"It was very nice. We got to meet a lot of the elderly relatives whom we have not seen for years together. Also, we had to tend to some of the ancestral property dealings."

Mrs. Lakshmi Narayan nodded her head satisfactorily as she finished her last sip of the coffee. Geethanjali came forward to take the coffee cup and saucer from her hands.

"Thanks! Geetha," she nodded again. And then her attention shifted to Geetha. "So, Geetha did you also go away with your family on the trip or were you staying at the hospital? How was your hospital managing during the floods?"

"Actually Aunty, I am just back from Kerala today morning. I had been staying there for a month,"

"Kerala?"

"We are working on re-opening one of our branches there. I should have returned earlier, but because of the airport closures etc. I had extended my trip there to return after Amma and Appa came back home."

"Oh good,"

"But over here the hospital was open and working to some extent. Most of our staff live extremely close by so they were able to make it."

At that moment a cry came floating through the windows of the living room, "LAKSHMI...LAKSHMI..,"

"It's my husband calling. I must be going now," Mrs. Lakshmi Narayan got up hurriedly.

Geethanjali and the mom walked their neighbor to the entrance. Geethanjali loitered a little longer at the front gate and peered up at the sky. It was bright blue and sunny. Thankfully it is all ended she thought oblivious of the fact that she was in the eye of the storm that was going to brew over in her very home.

She walked back into the living room to hear her sister proclaim, "See Appa... It was due to the brilliant idea of my mother-in-law to go on a native village tour, that all of us escaped the havoc of the floods."

"Oh yes...," smiled back her father and mother, amused by their daughter's constant chirping of her mother-in-law's glories even in the smallest of things.

Geetha borrowed the morning papers from her father to skim through it. She unconsciously went to the weather section of the newspaper. And then her being quivered. She felt like a lone lost child trapped in the meandering desert plains as both thunder and lightning loomed large on the horizon as she took in the words of her sister.

"Amma... my mother-in-law inquired again today as to the answer she should give to her friend about the alliance. She is wondering why we are still dillydallying without giving our consent,"

"What? What is she referring to?" asked a shocked Geetha turning towards her parents.

"I had clearly stated it was a NO that very day even before they landed. But i just went through the façade only due to her pleas. So why were we waiting to say that we were not interested?"

"Geetha, we cannot be so hasty. We need to consider the merits of this alliance." her mom gently interrupted

"The groom is a good friend of Renuka's mother-in-law. She is full of warm recommendations for this alliance." her father continued.

"Appa...," murmured Geetha, her shock only growing further. Was it, history repeating itself? He had got her married to one Mr. Ashok due to some recommendations from his brother and he was again talking in the same vein.

"Geetha...," he countered, "I agree the age difference may be a little on the higher range., But there are many such successful couples. And how long can you keep going on like this? We're growing old too. And you need to surely settle down. We need to keep an open mind."

"Are you concerned by the kids?" interjected her mother gently again.

"Oh gosh... I cannot believe that we are discussing this as even something worth discussing. "

"Well it will be easier to take care of them since they are pretty grown-up," interrupted Renuka and continued, "They apparently have quite some offers but because of my mother-in-law's recommendation they are giving you first preference."

"Well tell them thanks. But no thanks. They can go to the next choice in the list."

"Geetha do not be so thankless and rude.... And as I said, how long can you keep on going like this? We need to keep an open mind. You need to keep an open mind. You need to be practical."

"Appa.... The issue is not whether I can go on like this forever or not. I'm not against marriage or re-marriage too. The issue is that if I choose to get married again it needs to someone worth marrying and caring for. I have wasted three precious years of my life locked in marriage with a person straight from some kind of torture land in the guise of marriage. And now I am thankful that I am free from it all. And I do not have any more years or months or weeks or days to be drowned in that helpless despair."

"And how my dear big sister, are you going to test these grooms if they are worthy and noble of asking for your hand?" challenged Renuka in a mocking tone.

"Renuka... let it be...," interrupted her father, "So, Geetha, you are saying that you need someone better?"

"Yes, appa... she says someone better, someone like Ryan

or maybe Ryan himself!"

Eerie seconds of silence ensued.

"Oh, my goodness!" gasped Geetha breaking the silence and thrown off guard.

"Why are you dragging my friend into this argument?"

"Oh good. Friend! It better, remain that way. Because if you had other ideas, please drop them."

"Renuka that's enough," intervened her mother trying to stop the argument between the sisters.

"No, amma. We need to discuss it. We need to put a fool stop to her friendship with him. She is blindly refusing proposals or talking big only because of him and his interference. Did we not see the smiles on their faces and eyes sparkling even brighter than almost all the lighting in our wedding hall,"

For a fleeting second, Geetha recalled her friend in that memorable evening in her life. Yes, it was memorable to her since she had had a wonderful time that evening. It was memorable since that had been her first evening in her life after her divorce officially when she had faced her entire troupe of relatives and family friends, not with one sense of awkwardness due to her marital state, but with confidence and peace. And yes, it was true his presence and company was the pillar that she had leaned on. In fact, probably he was the pillar that propped her and made her ready to face her entire life on her terms. How could her sister admonish him and her friendship with him? And she surely did not deserve him for a brother-in-law!

With studied calm she replied, "to reiterate again, we were just good friends, and..,"

"Alright Geetha, that's enough. Now, let's discuss what we need to answer the alliance on hand …," her father interrupted impatiently fearing the direction the discussion was taking.

"Wait Appa, I have not finished answering her…she is the one who is taking this talk on a tangent. But come to think of it, Ryan my friend, is actually a perfect example of a person any father should be happy and proud to have his daughter marry…,"

"Geetha, I told you not to entertain any such thoughts," roared her father his temper rising. He hoped that this daughter would be suppressed by his glowering looks. He recalled how his little adamant Geetha had always finally given in when he had put on his angry mask.

But this was a new Geethanjali that he was seeing, some-one firmly believing in herself and articulating her position and asserting her rights to live on her terms calmly which was disturbing to the senses of her parents. How could they argue with her when what she said made sense?

Thus, this Geethanjali unfazed by the glowering looks bestowed on her continued,

"Well, what's so claustrophobic about Ryan?"

She waited for a whole minute for a response before continuing,

"I'm not going to turn away arguments against him by saying that he is not a dinosaur from the pre-historic days or not the alien from outer space."

"Neither am I going to say that he belongs to the same human species or that he has the same number of systems, bones, tissues, nerve pathways or cells like all of us."

"Think Appa...Think...,"

"Here's a hint. I was married to somebody who belonged completely to the same culture, sect, same set of practices and even was a distant relative."

She turned towards her mother, "Amma, do you recall your Aunt's 60th wedding celebrations function when you saw me, maybe a few days after my marriage. I was standing there dressed like a new bride, as expected with all my jewelry and fine silk saree. But do you remember what the many relatives questioned you later during that function,"

Mrs Vasudevan tried hard to think back At first, she was at a loss. And then it came back flowing to her. With a start she realized what her daughter was trying to say. How could she as a mother, forget that evening?

How many relatives had casually commented to her that her daughter appeared to look so dull and listless. And when she had broached the question later to her daughter it was the first evening that her dear daughter had lied to her. It was the first evening that she acted all grown up and said that all was well and she was just having a headache. It was the first evening when as a mother she had sensed that all was not well in her new home.

She looked up to see her daughter still looking at her. "Was I even able to manage a plastic smile successfully those days without you reading into it?"

"And now Renuka jokes that our smiles were even brighter than the scores of lights adorning the reception hall. It was possible because of our friendship which was made possible by our same underlying values and principles and interests etc. Same culture and practices were not a recipe for happiness. It all depends on the underlying principles and values with which one's parent's raises us irrespective of the latitude or longitude of where our homes are located."

"It is not practical. We all live as a part of the society and need to conform to certain norms."

"Well appa, you, me, amma and Renuka are all part of this society. But if we do not take the first step to think about it or adapt for progressive changes how can we claim that society will not change? And what are we doing, which is against the society? Surely society will not grudge a person to be happy for the right reasons. We're just saying that it's having values and principles in common that count. I'm just saying that one should not blindly deride someone or blindly advocate for someone."

The pressure cooker chose to whistle from the kitchen at that time. And Mrs Vasudevan thankfully scurried away with an excuse to exit the discussion.

Geetha turned toward the remaining folks.

"Think Appa. Just put on your thinking cap."

And then with a sudden broad smile she added and sealed the debate for that morning, "Do not take any decisions using your Amygdala. Use your prefrontal cortex."

36

OH AUNTY...

A SLIGHTLY MENTALLY exhausted Geetha trudged up the second floor stairs of her Aunt's apartment. She mechanically pressed the doorbell. As she stood waiting at the door, she replayed the happenings in her home just an hour ago.

"Did she speak too much?" she wondered. Two months had almost passed by since he had left the country and ever since then she had not heard a word from him. And here, her folks were harping about him as being the cause for matters of her heart. She was interrupted by her thoughts by the clanging sound of the gas cylinder delivery boy. She realized that her aunt had not yet responded and worried.

She knocked on the door calling, "Aunty...it's only me Geetha,"

"Coming..." she heard a voice from within and stopped worrying and went back to replaying the morning events.

"Oh, why did it have to happen? How could she have avoided it?"

And then she remembered her friend's favorite words of wisdom and smiled,

"Whatever happens or has happened is for the good.

Whatever is happening now is also happening well.

And whatever will happen will also happen well....,"

She peeked through the balcony where she was standing and shot a look up at the sky and smilingly thought.

"Well Dr. Ryan what would you say now if you heard this? How would you justify the happenings now? What is so well that is happening now"

And then she became aware of a loud hiccup from her. She pulled her water bottle out of her handbag and began sipping it. She continued to sip and continued to think.

"Maybe you would justify that I had enlightened my parents about the amygdala and prefrontal cortex?"

The door opened and a mentally exhausted niece greeted a tired looking Aunt.

"Come on in, Geetha... The bell never rang. We have low voltage still. Major power fluctuations..."

"Power is still not fully restored properly...," her Aunt continued further.

"Oh... So how are you now aunty?"

"Going on, Geetha."

"How did you manage aunty? None of us were here in town to be of any help."

"Oh well... I was feeling like a Rapunzel in a second floor

apartment," her Aunt joked

"Oh Aunty...," Geetha understood the pain behind those words.

"What to do Geetha? I must admit it was pretty trying. No drinking water, no power, no phone connection, no help. It was pretty depressing. I was left wondering that I had pledged to donate all my organs but what use will anything be if people are not able to come on time...,"

"Oh Aunty...no..."

"It's times like these when loneliness is very painful and frightening and everything is so uncertain,"

"And that's why Geetha ...you need to look at settling down too.... No man or woman is an island..."

"Aunty???" looked up Geetha. This was becoming even more mentally stressful.

"I was just off the phone with your father. He told me all that had happened today,"

"Oh...," understood Geetha.

"Nobody told you to marry any Tom, Dick or Harry.... But when the right person comes along please promise to not turn it down...,"

"Aunty... Has the cook come today? Let me help prepare something," the niece said wishing to divert the subject.

"Oh, that's ok Geetha. She came in today. Maybe you can help open the new medicine bottle for me. It's behaving a little too stubborn for me," she said her cheery countenance returning thankfully, pointing to the bottle on the dining table,

Geetha opened the bottle and her Aunt took a pill out of it and swallowed it with some water.

"I have another bottle too Geetha, inside the bedroom dresser."

And then Geetha's hiccups returned.

"Drink Geetha," her Aunt passed a glass to her,

Geetha gulped down some water. For a moment it seemed to have stopped. But then it again resurfaced even more louder and stronger than before. Geetha reached out for some water from the jug on the table. But it did not appear to subside.

"Have something to eat too Geetha. It would be surely better than,"

"Oh okay Aunty," she let out a ginormous hiccup. Feeling self-conscious she hurriedly helped herself to some cookies.

"Probably someone is thinking of you...," joked her Aunty.

"Oh...," smiled Geetha. She remembered that there was an old tale that when you get a hiccup consistently, it probably meant that someone was thinking of you in your absence. Well her mother and father must be discussing her outburst still she thought sadly.

And then the next words from her aunt froze her and her hiccups stopped in the very next second.

"Probably it is Ryan,"

She stood transfixed quietly hoping for a tiny second that it indeed was true.

Does he ever think of her? Her thoughts wondered.

"See it stopped," she again heard her aunt's words bringing her back to reality, "it was a shock therapy Geetha." chuckled her aunt.

"Yes, indeed aunty. It worked." She smiled back walking to the medicine chest, "let me now get the bottle,"

She found the bottle and opened it and returned with it to her aunt.

"Have you not yet heard back from him Geetha?" gently enquired her Aunt.

"No Aunty...not me directly," the niece maintained her smile. "At the hospital, as a staff member I heard that he had settled back with his parents and had resigned his position here."

"Have you not tried to reach him Geetha?"

"I did email him that very day when he left, to the email ID on his records with the hospital. But it just bounced back. Also, there was one contact number in the file and I did try that too. But someone else responded and was not aware of Ryan in anyways and just said that it was a wrong number. But he has my number. He could have reached me if he had wanted."

"Any news of him returning... Maybe to settle his things here...?"

"No aunty,"

"And you are still holding a torch for him Geetha???"

An awkward pause ensued for a whole minute. And then it was Geetha's turn to pose a question to her Aunt.

"Aunty... Why are we all born here in this earth...? Or rather what's the purpose of life?"

"Geetha...." Her aunt hesitated. What were the thoughts flowing in her niece's head? The niece did not expect the aunt to answer the question. Geethanjali herself volunteered,

"Aunty... as a school child I recall reading these particular lines of a poem..."

"All the world's a stage. Men may come and men may go..."

The aunt nodded slowly.

"Well aunty... I do not pretend to know the real essence of life. But when I come and go, I do not want to merely come and go. I want to come and go happily."

The Aunt continued to nod as her niece continued,

"I know that during the time that I was trapped in my marriage, I used to feel so disgusted with myself as to the life I was leading. I used to wish for the earth to open up and swallow me. There were so many visits to the temple I made when I used to cry my heart out.

But now, during the last 10 months, it's like I'm finding myself –a much better and real me back again. I have started feeling life and living life again.

Ryan was somehow a part of this journey where he elevated me to taste my capabilities. Or maybe, very simply stated he brought back the smile to my face,

"Of course, it is a little painful that he is not there since I had got too accustomed to him.

But I am still smiling, maybe not deliriously happy, but still happy and confident, that I can take everything in my stride."

Mrs. Shyamala Sundaram thus watched her niece quietly as she thus poured out her heart. She re-called eleven months ago that she had advised her niece to take baby steps to get back on her feet and face the world, but now she had certainly taken giant strides.

What could she do to help she meditated and then got up with an excited start.

She scurried inside her bedroom.

"Wow," thought Geetha. Her aunt's gait seemed to be

improving day by day. Ryan's treatment must be working really well, she smiled.

The Aunt noticed her niece smiling to herself as she emerged back from the bedroom carrying her diary.

"What happened Geetha?" asked the Aunt flipping through the pages.

"Aunty ...you actually look well...now"

"Oh, I just took my medicine..."

"Did you have them during the floods ..."

"Not really Geetha...I guess my routine was totally affected and I quite forgot about my medicines etc...,"

"Well Aunty if you had been feeling so well, would you have felt so helpless during those floods?"

"Oh ...maybe not so helpless...,"

"So, guess Aunty...it's not loneliness which we need to worry about ...the real problem is health."

"Well...Geetha..."

"If one is healthy, we can overcome all other issues...,"

"Wow ...you are marketing me your Health Buddy as the sole buddy needed!"

"Well Aunty...!"

"Oh, I was kidding Geetha," broke the Aunt into a huge grin as she finally stopped flipping the pages and came across the page she was looking for.

"Geetha...," continued her Aunt, her face glowing as if she was on the verge of decoding the characters on a treasure map. "I do not have a crystal ball to predict the future. Let whatever happen...happen. But do not give up without trying. And you surely need to always hold on to this friendship."

Saying, she pushed the open diary under Geetha's nose.

Geetha slowly read what she was pointing at. The niece stood excited but speechless. It was the phone number of Ryan's Aunt!

And at the same time,

p a a d a v a a   p a a d a v a a ...

rang out Geetha's phone.

She saw the same strange number again on her display -the one she had been receiving for the past few days...the number which she had seen quite some times in Kerala. She had thought it was a state network specific message and had ignored it, but now it is again coming in Chennai too?

"Wow ...the same fancy number again +123456789...,"

"Wait Geetha, what number did you say?"

"It says +123456789..."

"Hey, I think that is an International number. It could be an International number from an international calling card. Could it be Ryan?"

For a moment Geetha missed a heartbeat. A renewed sense of hope enveloped her.

37

LET'S JOIN THE BOAT PARADE

RYAN FINALLY loaded the last container of the anti-freezing liquid into the barrel and started slowly wheeling it towards the dock. He was quite surprised to see the marina brimming with people dressed in festively and eager chatter.

He anticipated spending a quiet winter morning in the marina, but it did not look to be so.

He had probably never seen that many folks even on a bright summer day.

"Anything special today?" He questioned to one of the staff of the marina.

"Oh, today afternoon, we will be having a bonfire and carol singing and will be then joining the boat parade."

"That sounds fun. Thanks for the info," smiled Ryan.

He mechanically smiled and greeted the other folks he

crossed on his way to the dock as he wheeled the barrow towards his boat slip.

And then for a moment he registered his surroundings and genuinely smiled when he spotted his boat's flag sailing tall.

"Ah dear boat...,"

But then his thoughts again became a little restless as he listlessly made his way to the boat.

"Concentrate Ryan," he chided himself

He had reached the dear boat of his dear parents. He was there that morning to winterize their boat. It was actually a pleasant winter Sunday morning and his mother had wanted to do something fun outdoors. His father had regained all the strength and zest for life and had also expressed the same wish. But Ryan had other thoughts invading his mind and thus had come up with a strange idea that he needed to go winterize their boat on the pretext to get some quiet time all by himself. He unloaded the last of the containers of the anti-freezing liquid and plopped himself onto the seat and again flipped open his phone.

He browsed again through the twitter updates on the Chennai floods. Well, nothing new. It will be late evening there. So, guess no new updates, he thought. He feverishly prayed for probably the nth time, "Oh God let she and her family be safe."

He had tried calling her many times ever since he had heard about the floods, but his calls had not gone through. And then his phone rang loud and clear as if in response to his prayers.

"Hello Aunty," answered Ryan dully.

"Hey Ryan!" sounded the excited voice of his aunt.

"What's up Aunty? How's the shopping going?"

"Oh, it's going fabulous. Your mom is indulging quite a bit. And your dad is also having a blast.

"Good," smiled Ryan and mechanically in parallel again opened the twitter updates on the Chennai floods.

"Hey Ryan... Guess, what...I received a call..,"

And then his hands almost dropped the phone when he heard the next words from his aunt,

"Ryan... I received a call from Geetha!"

"Geetha...!!! which Geetha...???" Was he hallucinating now he wondered. Had he heard correctly?

"Your Geetha," she began answering and then laughing corrected it, "our friend Geethanjali from Chennai,"

"I did tell her that we had read about those historic floods in the news and that we had tried contacting them. She said that she had been on a visit to Kerala for some hospital work and that her parents had gone to their native town. Only her Aunt had to face the brunt of the floods.

"Oh..." said Ryan hanging on to every word she said as his mind worked overtime in varied deductions. She's only talking of herself and her parents thought Ryan. So, she surely is not married yet. Thank you, God for keeping her and her folks all fine, he dropped a quick message to God.

"And thank you aunty,"

"All right, Ryan. I got to go. I see some interesting sales posted in this shop."

"Oh aunty, why don't we also go sailing today? There's a boat parade setting out from the marina in the afternoon and we could all join them."

"Wow we would love to! And whom do we owe to for the sudden change of mind?" teased his aunt.

"Anyways, down by the docks in 2 hours," chuckled his aunt and ended the call.

"Aah, thank you God.... I troubled you quite a bit!" he smiled pensively. He had just been hoping for her safety. But God seem to have returned his friend too to him. With renewed bouts of energy and contentment he set about getting the boat ready for the afternoon rendezvous.

For the first time that morning he became aware of the eight- legged arachnids swarming in the outside deck and under the bimini covers.

"Ouch!" He jumped as he saw that one had actually been comfortably housing itself in his coat for quite some time. "Ahh...you pesky creatures," he smiled, "you need to find a different home,".

And then he slowly repeated his aunt's words and smiled. "Your Geetha..."

Joy and festivity reigned supreme in the air.

38

CHRISTMAS GIFTS

GEETHA STROLLED around the empty garden in the Orphanage Home, smiling and humming to herself. The air was cool. The skies were clear. There were a few puddles of water here and there which were the only signs of the floods that had ravaged the city.

She stopped her humming as two men came in carrying a table. They were going to place the table in the usual area where generally the meetings used to be held in the past.

"Oh no...let's place it over here instead. There's water there." Geetha redirected them.

The table was placed as requested in the new place.

"Anything else, Madam?"

"That would be all. Thank You,"

Sathish came in slowly, carrying 2 oversized heavy bags.

He placed it on the table.

"Thanks, Sathish,"

"You are welcome Akka,"

Geetha began humming and she started scooping out the packages from the 2 bags.

"Wow Akka ...you look so happy. Anybody would think all these gifts are for you,"

Geetha just continued to smile, her eyes sparkling with contentment and peace as she picked up the carefully packed packages and placed them on the table.

Was that the sole reason for her huge smiles.

She turned her focus towards matching the gifts with the names of all the kids at the home.

"I had checked earlier, but just want to make sure that we are not missing anything for anybody."

"How did you come up with the specific gift ideas Akka?"

"Well Ryan and I had discussed the options based on what we have observed as the kids interests. And then I did the shopping, Of course even while shopping, he used to be on the phone and we used to finalize the choices."

"Wow!"

The bell rang and then those little children, her initial harbingers of hope trooped in. Their eyes widened in surprise, disbelief and excitement as they saw the packages neatly placed on the table. The warden also accompanied the children

"Akka, what is it? Is it all for us?" blurted out little Dhammu first.

Geetha continued to smile, managing a tiny nod but waiting for the warden to inform the children.

"Well children, all these gifts have been sponsored by Dr. Ryan Anna and his family. I will now call out your names and you can step forward to receive your gifts"

With eyes as bright as snow glazed tree tops, the little children collected their gifts from Geetha and Sathish as the warden then began to call out the names. The last name was called and the last gift was handed out.

The last of the gifts were given out. But strangely, none of the children had yet opened their gifts and instead just stood around Geetha and Sathish.

"What's up?" Geetha and Sathish exchanged looks.

"Akka, we were hoping that you could help us open the package carefully,"

"Oh, I can help...,"

"Carefully Sathish Anna, we want to preserve the gift wrap paper. It looks so colourful,"

"Oh...guess Geetha is the person then for the job, she wrapped it...she can peel out the tapes carefully...,"

"You can surely try too Sathish. Just be a little nimble and watch me do it first ...,"

"Alright children, let me do a few and show you how to do it," Gingerly Geetha began peeling out the cello tapes and the first package was opened .

A scream of delight rent the air," I got my own watercolors and acrylics paint set,"

"An encyclopedia on plants and a book on organic farming!"

"An astronaut costume and a book on space research!"

The warden walked away with an amused smile allowing the children to enjoy the opening of their gifts.

"I got my own Doctor's play kit."

"Can we try our costumes now?"

"Of course,"

Geetha helped the kids on with their costumes.

"Oh...let me take some pictures. Ryan wanted lots of them," Sathish flipped open his phone

"Actually Sathish, let's see if we can get into a video call with Ryan,"

"Would that not be too late for him Geetha Akka? I think it would be nearing midnight for him."

"That's quite true. But he said that he would be on night duty today. So, we are fine to call him,"

"Alright kiddos, all come forward. Let's try a video call to Ryan Anna,"

"Use your phone Sathish. Mine doesn't have those capabilities. It is pretty archaic,"

"Ah, when will you get rid of that old phone!"

"Well it is sufficient for it's basic functions of placing and answering calls,"

"Akka, my crown keeps slipping off," Mariam came forward.

"Oh...yes ...true...let's see if we can get a clip or a pin,"

"It will be in the office Akka,"

Geetha walked Mariam to the office and found a safety pin and carefully fastened the sides to ensure the crown fit her head correctly.

"Guess, I bought a slightly bigger size,"

"That's fine Akka, then only I can use it for many more years,"

"There it fits perfectly now,"

The little girl caught sight of her reflection on the glass window and paraded herself grandly in front of it...

"Ryan Anna! Ryan Anna!" cries from the garden floated through the window.

"Oh, the video call must have started,"

"Let's go Akka,"

"You carry on. I will put away this box and join all of you,"
The little girl scurried away.

Geetha carefully put away the box and walked amusedly towards the little excited party, just in time to see Sathish presenting Mariam to Ryan on the video call.

"And here comes our ruler ...the great Mariam!"

"Mariam came forward with a grand stride and produced a book with a giant flourish,"

"A book? Where's your sword ...thought you were a ruler,"

"I got a book only Sathish Anna...this is my encyclopedia,"
A chuckle was heard on the other side.

"Oh Sathish...that must be our Geetha's vision of a ruler... she thinks that rulers should leave their mark by creative contributions to mankind and should not indulge in warfare... so that must be her vision of a peaceful, knowledge based leader,"

Geetha stopped in her tracks and sat down on a bench abruptly. She wanted to savor that moment. A strange flutter passed through her being. He still remembers everything about me. Her eyes caught the colorful package wrappings spread on the table in from of her. She had got the gift that she had asked for herself. She had got back her friend.

39

FIVE MONTHS LATER

FIVE MONTHS later, the kitchen of Mrs. Vasudevan was invaded by her daughter in the wee hours of the morning. The aroma of fresh ghee permeated from the kitchen into the hall.

"Gosh whatever are you doing? You are making a huge mess!" pleaded her mother helplessly.

"Ah Amma .... Please do not come in until I say so!" her daughter peeked her head out of the kitchen.

"Geetha ...I need to prepare the breakfast. Your father will be soon down."

"Amma, I'm almost done. Another 10 minutes only please!" And then cheekily added, "enjoy the aroma, Amma!"

"Are you using ghee?" sniffed her mother again. "All right I will cut the vegetables now. But I need you to vacate the kitchen in 10 minutes as you promised."

"Hmmm..., Whatever has happened to her?" wondered her mother. She had been hearing noises from the kitchen for quite some time. She appeared to have taken refuge in the kitchen at least for a whole two hours churning out some secret dish.

And then true to her word, 10 minutes later a victorious Geetha emerged from the kitchen gingerly carrying a box of those secret goodies.

"Can I finally enter?" teased her mother with relief.

"Oh yes. I have cleaned it all up. It is all spick and span, waiting for my dear mother to make it messy again!"

"What? I make a mess while cooking?"

"Oh Amma...I was joking!"

"Oh goodness me," the mother entered the kitchen and gasped at the 2 ghee containers parked in the dust bin.

"You used 2 whole litres of ghee?" She cried in disbelief.

"Oh no Amma. One bottle was not full. So maybe just 1.5 litres of ghee."

And then like a consolation prize her daughter plated two of the secret goodies and offered them to her mom.

"These look like paniyarams. So, were these the secret goodies that you were churning out in the kitchen for such a long time?" her mom eyed them.

"Taste them first, Amma,"

Her Amma took a bite and rolled her eyes again in disbelief.

"These are indeed Paniyarams. But you fried them in ghee?" She cried in disbelief." You wasted so much of the pure cow ghee for frying rather than using the regular oil?"

"Yes, amma.... But aren't they a whole lot different? Aren't they straight out of heaven?" self- complemented Geetha.

"I've never said that cooking was your forte. I wonder who's going to get an achy tummy.? Ghee is so heavy,"

"Oh," her daughter looked disappointed.

"I was joking. So, who are they for?"

Geethanjali looked around and confirmed that her father was still nowhere in sight and whispered softly,

"For Ryan,"

"What?" her mom looked up again experiencing disbelief.

"Oh, but you said that he's not here, he had left many months ago?"

"Oh yes, amma. But he had a seminar to attend and present a paper on. And he is in Chennai just for today.

"Just one day?" clarified her mother.

"Yes, amma. In fact, he had some pending exams for Siddha and Ayurveda which he gave in Delhi and came to Chennai too to attend the seminar. So quite a short and hectic schedule,"

"Well, all that I can say is, I do not remember you ever attempting to cook any such dish for any of us."

"Well, Amma not to worry, I will make these for your next wedding anniversary!"

"But, amma are these paniyarams really not nice? They are made of ghee and surely anything made of ghee should be at least good, if not heavenly?" asked the daughter coming back to her question on the paniyaram taste.

"Well," smiled her mother amusedly. She was not sure if it did taste heavenly. But there was some special exquisite ingredient which made it stand out.

"I will ask him to eat it after he lands back in US. Since it is made of ghee it surely will not go stale."

40

WHAT IS IT?

GEETHA WAS on her last official chore of the day. She was sitting in the waiting section of the bank to hand over some statements on operations which the bank had requested from her hospital.

Geetha's eyes subconsciously searched for the clock hanging in the far end of the room. The day was seeming to move exceptionally slowly. She probably flipped open her phone for the 150th time for that day to confirm the time.

Hmmm... The earth must be taking an extra long time to rotate around the sun today. Or is it also nervous? She mused.

"Amma[23].... Can you please help me fill up this deposit challan?" An old lady requested Geetha the interrupting

23 Amma-Ma'am (respectful usage to a lady in Tamil language)

her thoughts.

"Oh sure," said Geethanjali glad to do something to bide her time.

She filled up the challan and handed it over to her.

"Thank you Amma," smiled the old lady.

She again watched the clock. Same as the one in the hospital she thought. Her eyes then fell across the paintings adorning the wall. They were just representations of the rainbow from different perspectives. Hmmm... So nice and pleasing to the senses. It's been quite some years since I've seen a real rainbow she thought.

Then her eyes darted across the certificates hanging on the wall. It was the bank's registration certificate. Another was the building inspection certificate.

Oh gosh wait Ms. Geethanjali... Have I come here for the bank inspection now? She smiled at herself.

"Token 50," sounded the bank announcement.

Oh good. My turn would be next, she thought. But then a sudden sense of anxiety blew over.

Actually I'm pretty observant today. But they say that love is blind. What gasped her mind? Had she used the word "Love?". Oh no, he is just a friend she thought nervously. Of course, he's just a friend her mind reassured her. Possibly you are in love with love. You do not necessarily need to to be in love with him, the heart too tried to comfort her.

Oh I need to put away these thoughts, she tried to steady herself. She walked over back to the wall where the certificate of inspection of the building hung and feverishly began reading it. And was mighty glad when she saw her token number flashing on the electronic counter.

"Good evening Ms. Geethanjali," the bank senior loan officer greeted her.

"Good evening Sir!"

She was there to just hand over some statements that the bank had requested for. The manager quickly browsed through it and fixed his rubberstamp on it and then and then began rummaging the files on his desk. He appeared to be missing something.

"My pen? Wherever did it go?" He murmured. He then reached out to his colleague, "Sakunthala Madam, please pass me a pen,"

"Is that the pen you are looking for, Sir?" interrupted a helpful Geetha pointing to a golden fountain pen peeping through one of the files.

"Ah yes yes! I was actually searching for the specific pen since this morning!"

He grandly signed the documents with a flourish. "Thanks Ms. Geethanjali!"

"You're welcome!" Geetha smiled back.

A few minutes later she finally exited the bank and hailed a passing auto rickshaw.

"To Dr. Radhakrishnan road, "

"Yes ma'am, please get in!"

As soon as auto rickshaw kick started, her thoughts too kick started into motion. They say that absence makes the heart fonder, would that have had any impact on him?

"Oh no!" She almost bellowed that the auto driver turned back startled,

"Anything the matter? Not this road?"

"Oh no... It's fine," she shook her head.

Enough, she chided her thoughts.

Concentrate on something else.... Maybe look at those cars zooming by! But nevertheless, she could not help being nervous as the auto neared the hotel. Will he be her old friend Ryan or would he have changed? Think, of something else, she again tried reprimanding and reminding herself. Well... the weather is so unusually pleasant today for an afternoon in the month of May. For a wee brief moment she looked up at the clouds dancing up above the sky. Would it, next rain too? Well that would be the wonder of wonders. Or were they simply peeping down out of curiosity to see what was going to unfold in her life.

41

THE SEMINAR IS OVER AND...

"Wow ... finally at last!" noted a happy Ryan when the last final presentation of the seminar ended. Generally, he would have hung back interacting with the other attendees and would probably have been one of the last persons to leave the seminar hall. But not today. He was all packed up.

He did have many thoughts and many questions on some of the presentations. But no, he was not going to ask them that evening. He was not going to do anything which would delay him. He literally shot out of his seat, grabbed his bag and was the first person to be out of the seminar hall.

"No questions today Dr. Ryan?" joked another attendee as he passed him.

"Oh nopes, Sir crystal-clear," smiled back Ryan.

"Hmmm...I did not find it so clear. I still have quite some

doubts...I was in fact waiting for Dr. Ryan to raise them first," that man pondered as Ryan breezed past him.

There were bigger questions plaguing Dr. Ryan's mind. Will he be seeing her soon? Or would she not be able to make it? Did she consider him only as a friend or was it something more? Even if she knew it was something more, would she acknowledge it? Or will it be the last time that he was going to see her?

He dashed to the elevators, happy to see it available immediately.

He turned on his cell phone from the meeting mode and checked his voicemail.

The taxi to take him to the airport had been dispatched.

He put back away his phone. He watched the numbers display on the elevator mechanically.

Ground Floor, the elevator doors opened.

Hopefully he would get to see her today even if it was going to be rushed, he thought as he walked out of the elevator.

And then his thoughts froze for a moment. Just live in the moment. Do not trouble yourself with questions appeased his mind. There she was smiling and waving out to him and walking towards him. He slowly raised his hands wanting to embrace her. This was the smile and friend that he had become so accustomed to in the last year. All that he had dearly missed came flooding out of different pockets of memories in his brain.

"Oh," he realized what he was going to do and checked himself, abruptly pretending to shake away some invisible insect and instead held out his hand for a handshake as they neared each other.

42

HELLO...AGAIN...

Yesterday he did not know her...
Yesterday she did not know him...
Today he liked her...
Today she liked him...
Tomorrow will he be her memory?
Tomorrow will she be his memory?

They both shook their hands solemnly in strange, thoughtful silence before bouncing back to reality.

"So how have you been?" Ryan was the first one to question.

Waiting for you to come back, she wanted to answer, instead simply said,

"Doing fine,"

"So how have you been?" She counter questioned.

Hoping to see you waiting for me, he wanted to answer, instead said,

"Doing great!"

"So how was the seminar?"

"It was good...quite a bit of groundbreaking information,"

And then his phone rang. It was the taxi driver reporting that he had arrived.

"Oh, so early? What time is your flight" queried Geetha as he hung up the call.

"My flight is at 8 PM,"

"8 pm? Then I suppose, it is best to start now. The evening peak time traffic will soon start," she calculated.

"Oh, do not worry. I planned for us to get something at the coffee shop here in this hotel. That will be the only place for having a quick snack at this hotel."

"But Ryan... I do not think that is advisable,"

"Oh no Geetha...it's alright. I have already done the online check in. I also have my luggage all packed and ready with me." He said pointing to his carry-on luggage.

"It would be sufficient if I leave after an hour."

"Oh 1 hour...are you sure,"

"This way, please," guided the waiter as they entered the coffee shop and walked them to a table.

"Can we actually sit somewhere with a nice view?" asked Ryan scanning the tables.

"Actually, how about that table?" interjected Geetha pointing to a particular table near the water fountain,

"There are some fishes there too," whispered Geetha to Ryan.

"Yes, certainly Mam," smiled the waiter.

"Good choice," smiled Ryan as they settled down at the table. "And, when did you become a fan of the fish tribe?"

"Oh, just like that,"

"Hey actually I believe, water should flow down the through the rocks too once the water fountain is on, but it does not appear to be switched on yet,"

"Naturally Ryan, we are the only folks here ...maybe they would turn it on as the crowd picks up,"

"I suppose so. The pianist is also missing," he pointed to the empty piano.

A giant gold gilded menu card was placed before Ryan and Geetha.

"What will be the quickest to order?"

"Icecream, Mam...,"

"Wow... I never knew that there were so many icecream choices." Geetha's eyes popped out.

"Very interesting combinations," mused Ryan as he slowly began reading the first choice.

"Well Ryan, If we are going to be reading through all these, your plane will be surely taxing the runway without you...,"

"We have 1 hour Geetha...," he tried reassuring her.

"That was 10 minutes ago Ryan... Actually 12 minutes ago...," she pointed out staring at the time on her phone.

"Well, you seem to be mighty interested in packing me off quickly!"

"Well, you are the one who seems to have this jet rocket schedule,"

"All right, all right do not stare like that now...,"

Turning to the waiter he asked, "What is today's ice cream

special?"

"Rainbow dreams is actually our new super special creation being debuted this week,"

"Wow sounds colourful, but what's so super special about it?"

"Sir, it promises to provide seven different tastes to satiate your taste buds and we have a couple of promotions around it which is ending this evening at 6o' clock. So, you would be able to participate in that too"

"Well, I have heard of six different tastes, what's this seventh taste?"

"Happiness, Sir!"

"Oh My...,"

"Alright Ryan let's place the order without delaying," interrupted Geetha glaring at why he was wasting his time in chatting.

"Oh, wait Geetha...one sec...and so what are these ingredients?"

"Well that's the first promotion contest Sir. Whoever identifies the 6 key ingredients this week on it's opening debut, would win 3 gallons of icecream."

"And the second contest?"

"Whoever provides the best feedback will win a year's worth of ice cream."

"Wow, this sure sounds one super special icecream. We will have 2 please."

"And please make it quick,"

"Certainly Mam, just 1 minute," and he zoomed off with the menu cards.

"Oh Geetha, as I said we have time...,"

"Well Mr. Ryan ...it was you who came up with this race against time. You could have stayed back surely for a couple of days when you have come all the way so far."

"It was actually my brother-in-law who booked the flight," he responded knowing it did sound a bit too strange.

.   How could he admit that it was him who had given specific instructions to his brother-in-law to book the first possible flight out of Chennai. It was actually many months ago when he had not heard back from her. He had dreaded coming back to Chennai, he could not bear the possibility of her coming to meet him hand in tow with another person. He shuddered still at that thought. Maybe, I was acting from my amygdala and not from my prefrontal cortex, he sheepishly introspected. And then the ice cream treats arrived.

"Enjoy Sir, Enjoy Mam!" the waiter's voice sounded interrupting his thoughts.

"That really was a minute," exclaimed Geetha.

"There you go, Ms. Timekeeper!" started laughing Ryan conjuring up an image of Geetha with a clock and gong in hand.

"Oh." she wanted to glare back but burst out laughing too.

"All right, Ryan, let's finally celebrate!"

"Finally?"

"Oh, do you not recall Ryan..., We had planned to celebrate, but then you had to leave that night,"

"Ah yes, actually it was you who had first vanished that afternoon,"

"Well, I had vanished just for a few hours. But it was you who vanished without a trace for many months....and now again you will be ...," Her voice faded dully. She looked up and for a few moments her eyes met his eyes, both searching for clues in the other, but both masterfully concealing the emotions of their soul.

"Do you want me to stay?" his eyes were about to signal, but instead his usual twinkling eyes put up an extra special nonchalant gaze. He did not want to loose her friendship or offend her in any way if she mistook him.

"Stay," her eyes wanted to plead, but instead she put up a smiling front. She was thankful for his friendship and could not ask for more.

The few seconds of silence were unmuted by the sudden sound of water gushing through the rocks by their side. The fountain had been turned on earlier than it's regular scheduled time, apparently for Geetha's sake.

"Thank you!" She smiled in the direction of the waiter and he nodded.

"And look Ryan!" She gleefully pointed to all the fish swimming towards their side.

"Coming for your ice cream!" quipped Ryan.

"Well, they are all congregating in one place, looks like they are having their own celebration party too," she smiled back lost in observing them for a few moments.

She turned back towards Ryan just in time to see him hand over a scribbled note to the waiter.

"Oh, what happened Ryan?"

"Well let's celebrate,"

"Well our Health Buddy is already a huge runaway success and we are now working on it's second version ...so that's old news,"

"Oh well, no need of any special reason...let's just celebrate for everything in general,"

She nodded and they both scooped their first spoon.

"I just can't wait to taste this. It looks so heavenly!" she smiled eyeing which side she should first try out. True to it's name, it was a rainbow of colors.

She lifted her spoon towards her mouth waiting to be transported to a world of flavor and happiness.

But instead she dropped her spoon in horror. Her ears were most certainly playing a trick, she hoped. Maybe it was a different song she hoped. But no, she could recognize it. Wherever did this pianist now come from?. Why on earth did he need to pick this as his first song to play for the evening . She slowly turned towards her opposite chair, expecting it to have been abandoned by Ryan. But lo behold, it was another surprise for her. There, he was very much seated tight on his seat ...with a sweet countenance and his head swaying and nodding slowly as if it was lost in his most favorite music. He caught her looking and his eyes began twinkling.

"Did you think I will bolt away again?" it appeared to tease.

"This is Fur Eliste, ...the first song that I played on the piano. My most favorite song. I used to play it with my mom on many evenings,"

"Oh,"

"That's why I had asked this as the song request,"

"Oh it was you, who requested it!" Geetha sat even more dazed at what was happening

The song ended. Ryan got up and gave the pianist his resounding applause. Geetha amusedly, gave up trying to fathom her friend's transformation and instead began relishing her ice cream.

Thank you Geetha! Thank you for giving me back my music. Thank you for giving me back my happy memories! his thoughts thanked her within him.

"Oh Geetha, did I mention that my parents are considering to upgrade their boat?"

"Oh yes, I recall you mentioning it in one of your earlier emails,"

"Yes, then they were debating whether to do it or not... Looking at all the pros and cons... Now they have finally decided to take the plunge,"

"Oh nice....,"

"We need something more sea -worthy for the Atlantic Bahamas voyage they are planning,"

"Oh... That sure sounds adventurous...,"

"My sister and brother-in-law will be accompanying too. And my brother-in-law is a perfect capable captain. Our existing vessel was pretty good too, but this engine has even more power."

He logged onto his phone and pulled up a few pictures to show her.

"See these are the pictures of the boats we have narrowed our choices down to," and began sharing the detailed pictures of his boats. And then one picture led to another and soon he was sharing pictures of his working hospital, his routines, and she was sharing pictures of the new branch that they had opened in Kerala and her routines.

And they were suddenly jolted out of their world, as a voice quietly sounded.

"So how was the experience, Sir?" asked the waiter.

They both looked down at their icecream bowls. The silver bowls were all empty. They were not sure of what they had had. They were not sure if the rainbow dreams creation had added to their happiness on not. But they both sensed supreme happiness and contentment.

"We guess, we cannot answer for the ingredients," they both laughed.

"Feedback sir," the waiter pressed another feedback card to both of them.

And then as they became unconsciously aware that this happiness may soon be melting into just a happy memory, they absent-minded scribbled,

"Soulicious, " she scribbled.

"Soulicious," he scribbled.

43

IT'S GOODBYE...?

AND BEFORE long they were in the porte-cochère of the hotel.

"Let me drop you Geetha near the Mylapore tank. That's where you said you were going now."

They saw the taxi driver waiting impatiently for Ryan to get in as he held open the door.

"Come on Geetha. It's on the way."

"I don't think so Ryan," she refused and she could not help noticing the taxi man's disapproval of Ryan's idea. It would mean getting into Mylapore which again was traffic prone and would add up to his commute time.

And then a "BEEP!" behind them sounded. Cars were pulling up behind his taxi.

"Please Geetha," he insisted refusing to get in until she

got in too.

"BEEP," again the horn sounded.

That seemed to help her decide and she got into the car.

"Five extra signals, sir," she heard the driver muttering.

It was strange and painful to Geetha, getting into the car and sitting by him.

Yes, this may have brought them both some time, but the logical mind was only reminding them.

Just another 15 minutes he will be gone from her.

Just another 15 minutes and she will be gone from him.

Their thoughts which had been on hold in the last 45 minutes returned now with full force. And then they both again made a pact with their thoughts. We have plenty of time to brood and think later on. Let's just live in the moment for now. Ryan broke the silence first.

"Hey Geetha, the weather looks so perfect today. Not like the hot, sultry summer days that you were writing to me about."

"True, it actually rained yesterday and again today afternoon too. So, it kind of cooled down the heat."

"Oh well, Mother Earth must have made it especially cool for my visit, to welcome me," he self-gloated,

"Well it looks like it may rain again," she said peering out of the window at the sky.

"Allright Ryan, please convey my regards to your parents and Aunt Agatha,"

"Oh certainly, Aunt Agatha is actually in Bahamas now. She was the one who fueled my parents found idea of sailing to the Bahamas."

"Wow her zeal and zest for seeing and experiencing new

places is amazing,"

"So how are your parents doing? How is your little sister?"

"Oh... little?" she grimaced,

He just smiled.

"Oh Geetha, I think we're nearing your place, Wherever, is the traffic that you mentioned about? We seem to have breezed past the signals" he suddenly winced.

"Yes," she too realized.

And Geetha made an additional entreaty to mother Earth.

"Mother Earth please slow down. You surely must be tired with rotating on your axis day and night without any rest. I know you cannot stop, but can you please rotate a little bit slowly."

And then she heard a whisper from Ryan, "Look at the front mirror. The driver is actually smiling. His grumpiness seems to have been won over by our conversation,"

"I cannot see Ryan from my position. Anyways, mother Earth will probably listen to you. You are the one who claimed that she cooled down Chennai just for your arrival right?" She teased him.

"What, request mother Earth to slow down her rotation?" he asked incredulously.

"Yes, Ryan do something for your share,"

"Maybe the gravitational pull...," He began to contemplate and then stopped as another incredulous idea came up to him, "rather than asking mother Earth to slow down her rotation, we just need to get the clocks in the airport to slow down,"

"And how to we do that?"

He smiled sheepishly. And then whether in answer to

Geetha's entreaty or Ryan's entreaty, the car actually came to a sudden stop and they both burst out laughing. Was it going to be their final laughter for the foreseeable future? A few more vehicles had piled up.

"It's a procession," the driver informed them. But again, he was not in his earlier grumpy self. He looked pretty calm. Possibly their banter had really awakened the happy self in him.

How much longer will the unknown forces and elements be at work to buy them some more time? The procession peacefully passed off and the car started moving along.

"Where do you want to get down Mam?" The driver politely asked as the car slowly cruised past the Mylapore-Mandavelli bus stand.

Did reality hit them both? Not yet. They were still in each other's happy presence.

"Bye-bye Ryan. Have a safe journey!" Geetha said getting ready to get down.

"Oh.. but were you not going to visit that Temple behind the tank? It looks like a lot of traffic in this road. It's going to take a lot of time to cross the road. Can we please turn into the right side lane?" he requested the driver.

"No sir, if we turn into that lane, it would take us a whole 30 minutes to get back into the main road. It is jampacked there," he dismissed the request apologetically.

The car rolled down to a stop.

"Ma'am please get down here,"

"But...," Ryan began again.

"It's okay Ryan." She said grabbing her hand bag and opening the car door. And then she realized thankfully.

Pulling out the box from her bag she literally pushed it into Ryan's hand.

"Hey, I made them... paniyarams," She started to say but a deafening horn drowned out her words A great big bus was right behind the car honking. Couldn't the bus go past them and go with the other lane. But no, the stubborn bus just wanted the little car to move out of that way.

"Ma'am... bus," the driver apologized.

She closed the door abruptly and stepped back onto the pavement. The car pulled away

44

IN THE BOX...

"Oh gosh, I could not say a proper bye bye," Ryan looked back through the window, but his view was blocked by the bus.

She was there 2 minutes ago and now she is not here. A lump hit his throat. He just shut his eyes.

A sudden static sound made him open his eyes in the very next second.

The driver was fiddling the radio stations finding some music to play.

"Nothing please," Ryan murmured

And then his eyes registered the box that he was holding in his hand.

So, whatever had she prepared for him on a working day?

He was eager to know.

He had often heard her say that she had no time or incli-nation to cook especially on working days. Ryan opened the box carefully. He was pleasantly surprised to see the sweet goodies that greeted him.

"Oh, those sweet small brown balls ... My favorite Pani-yarams! " the twinkle returned to his eyes. She remembers everything, he mused and smiled and slowly bit into the paniyaram.

The lump slowly eased from his throat.

He was no culinary connoisseur. And then did the mystery ingredient reveal itself? What did he sense? Was it just the ghee and the batter? Was it just the exquisite texture and the divine flavor that he sensed or did it hold the key to what lay down within the layers of her soul? Or did it reveal the exquisite affection that she held for him carefully wrapped in the layers of friendship?

45

BATTLE OF EMOTIONS

MEANWHILE, THE first thought that struck Geetha as she saw the car disappear was,

"Oh gosh! I missed telling him that it was all fried in ghee and he should preferably eat them after he lands in his destination." She pulled out her phone. I need to call him she thought. And then all her thoughts and emotions which she had kept bottled up came flowing out. Did she only miss telling him about the ghee in the paniyarams? Did she not miss sharing something even bigger? What about sharing her true feelings for him? "Oh, please don't be absurd now for God's sake," she literally shouted out.

"What...? Watch out!" She heard a voice bellowing behind her. She turned back and saw that she was almost just a few inches away from walking into the road side flower shop.

"Oh, so sorry," she mumbled and traced her steps painfully in the direction of the crosswalk. No, her legs were not aching, but her whole being was literally burning with anguish and sense of loss.

"Now calm down. Take a few deep slow breaths." a voice within her advised. Now where did she see those pranayama [24]lessons she wondered. Oh yes, it was at the Children's Home that she visited. She tried to recall the steps and slowly tied to inhale in deep breaths. And that appeared to do the trick as she regained her composure and walked slowly to the crosswalk.

And in the next few minutes, she did manage to reach the crosswalk. Oh, then the signals were not working, she realized with dismay. No traffic constable was also in sight. The traffic had worsened by many folds Not just worsened. It had become impassable. Vehicles of all shapes and sizes were sounding their horns, all impatient to have the first right of passage.

Oh, my goodness, Ryan luckily missed this traffic just by a few minutes. And that, now triggered a full blown traffic jam in her thought stream. It was probably a battle of thoughts between her amygdala and her prefrontal cortex.

Why did you not tell him?

Tell him what? another part of her stubbornly responded.

How could I?

Will that not be embarrassing?

Besides, why do I need to tell him anything?

Does he need me to say it in words explicitly?

Is it not a feeling? Did he not sense it?

---

24   pranayama - breathing

Well do not be ridiculous!

Oh, all right. But how could I be the one to say it?

Now which era of the Stone Age are you living in? It does not matter whether a man says it or whether the woman says it! Whoever gets the courage first can certainly say it.

Oh, I do agree with that. But the bigger issue is what if he just turns it down. If he just says that it was just friendship all along! Would it not be embarrassing to me and to him?

How he responds is his choice wholly. But how you manage your life is your choice.

It's just a question or feeling that you are sharing or expressing with that someone who you think is so special in your life.

If he says YES, then yes it will be all perfect. But if he says NO... so be it. Shed a few tears and move on.

At least this heavy question would be lifted from your heart. You will never be at least left with this regret that I lost without asking. At least I tried.

"Aren't you crossing, amma?" She heard an external voice asking her. She looked up and realized that quite a few pedestrians had piled up and were going to cross the road together.

"Oh, it's all right. Please carry on. Thanks." She dismissed and took a few steps backward into the pavement. She was not ready to cross yet. She needed to calm herself first. And possibly another old friend was also waiting to visit her. My friend ...The Tears!

No, she could not tear up in the middle of the road. She looked up at the sky for solace. Yes, there seemed to be a dark cloud hovering there. Oh God ... She shut her eyes wishing fervently. Please let it rain. Please let it rain. I can at least cry peacefully. She sent one last request for that day to Mother Nature.

And she slowly opened her eyes hoping to have her prayers answered. But no, that one big dark cloud too had mysteriously vanished revealing a clear blue canvas. And there was an even bigger surprise unfolding before our eyes. Whatever was it? Colors was slowly taking form.

She stood transfixed in the majesty of nature's performance. It was a rainbow. She had never seen one, so clear and huge for a very long time. Her soul was slowly clearing up.

And then she felt the warm grip of that hand that told it all.

46

YESTERDAY, TODAY, TOMORROW...

Looking up she saw the radiant face of her Ryan.

"Isn't it time that we decided to cross together?" he asked gently.

"Yes...," she nodded.

The traffic had no way lessened. Honks were still deafening the open skies. But the signal lights had started working. And suddenly not one, but two traffic constables were also seen running to take position at the intersection and regulate the traffic. Holding hands, they crossed the road.

Yesterday he did not know her...
Yesterday she did not know him...
Today he adored her...
Today she adored him...
Tomorrow he will be with her for eternity and sempiternity!
Tomorrow she will be with him for eternity and sempiternity!

"So how have you been?" he softly asked.

"Waiting for you to come back?" she blushed, "And how have you been?"

"Hoping to see you waiting for me," he admitted sheepishly.

"So, shall we celebrate?" they both asked.

"Icecreams again?" They both burst out laughing.

"Actually, I would like to go back to that hotel to taste that ice cream now and identify those ingredients now!"

"Actually, we need to get you back on track to the airport first. Do not forget that you still have a flight to catch,"

Little did they know, that they were soon going to be invaded by those very ice creams. At that moment, two shipping labels were being affixed on two shipment containers full of ice creams. They had won the "Rainbow Dreams" icecream promotion contest.

And a Note ……

Dear Reader,

We hope that we had you also smiling as you finished traversing the lives of the various characters as
they transformed their lives to reach their dreams.

Was there anything in particular or any specific
character that you enjoyed the most? We would be
so very happy to hear from you, if you could spare a
few more moments to leave a review of the book either
in goodreads.com or the digital retailer where you
chanced upon this book.

Regards,

FRom the Team working hard at promoting
Radiant SunshineReads: -)